BEACH SUNRISE

BEACH HOUSE ROMANCE
BOOK 1

JULIE CAROBINI

Beach Sunrise (Beach House Romance, Book 1)

JULIE CAROBINI writes inspirational beach romances from her home on the California coast. Please visit her at JulieCarobini.com.

ONCE UPON A TIME ...

I wrote a series about five siblings who inherited a beach house—with a catch!

That was in 2020 ... and we all know what happened *that* year. Life was turbulent so I decided to do something different: I released all five books under a pen name.

But ... I found it difficult to maintain two personas. Not sure why so many writers find this easy! I love my readers and simply found it difficult to be two people. *Does that make sense?*

I also wanted to add a bit more content to these stories. So I pulled the novels from publication, added new scenes, and re-covered the series under my own name.

If you like tropes, such as fake relationships, billionaires, secret babies, and cowboys, then I know you'll love the revised and refreshed Beach House Romance series!

Now, turn the page for book one ...

Julie

1

———————

Grace stepped into the office corridor, her heart beating in her ears. She may have spent the past several years studying law, but the last thing she wanted to do was wake up to a phone call from a ... lawyer. With a quick breath, she chased away the dregs of that early morning conversation, ran a hand down her skirt, lifted her chin, and stepped purposely into work.

She paused. The Law Offices of Ryan & Ryan usually hummed with energy—scratch that, they screeched.

But not today.

In the six days that Grace Holloway had toiled as a junior lawyer at this firm, a job that she had hunted down after weeks of disappointment, she'd already learned not to wince at the sounds of heated voices in the middle of tense negotiations. Especially those coming from far down the hall where the two lead attorneys of the firm wrestled over cases—and with each other.

Chase Ryan and Kate Little. Or as some around here said, *Chase and Kate*. They weren't a couple any longer, and though she personally found the idea of exes running a law firm together a little unusual, she admired the two for carrying it out.

A phone slammed against its base.

A grunt flew.

There it was—signs that though the office appeared empty, she was not alone. Her body tingled as if something had taken hold of her, and when she glanced down, she noted her hands were clenched so tightly her knuckles had turned white.

Despite all that, Grace bit her upper lip and stepped softly into her own small office, the one she shared with Mick, another new hire, who, like herself, thanked his lucky stars about once an hour that he had landed this job. She and Mick had bonded over coffee, bar exam horror stories, and her personal favorite—the number of resumes they had each submitted until finally being hired here.

She beat him one hundred and nine to his ninety-seven.

Grace glanced out the window, the smoggy Los Angeles day greeting her with a shrug. She fiddled with the potted plant on her credenza, then straightened the set of five classic books wedged between sea-inspired, vintage bookends. Other newly minted lawyers might prefer leather-bound law books in their offices. But if she was going to spend long hours here, likely missing meals and impromptu coffee dates with friends, she intended to make her space, small as it was, her own.

She glanced again at those whimsical bookends, her eyelashes fluttering at a memory made even more pronounced by the early morning wake-up call she'd received. The set was a gift from her mother after graduating from law school. The sea stars and shells made of blue cast iron cradled copies of *Jane Eyre*, *Little Women*, and *The Hiding Place*, among others, and evoked images of an underwater coral reef.

She swallowed back the sudden hitch in her throat at the thought of her mother ... her father, too. There were things she still had to do where her parents were concerned, but—she blew a sigh into the quiet—for now, duty called.

Grace seated herself in front of her desk and fired up her computer. She'd come in early to get a head start on the stack of files awaiting her and didn't dare ignore them any longer. The rumble from down the hall grew, but she opted to ignore it. Or try to.

A good half-hour passed interrupted only by something heavy landing against a wall. She jerked a look up. A note lay on her desk, the edges of the paper jagged, as if torn from a notepad in a hurry. How had she missed it? The handwriting was ... unmistakable. She had already learned to recognize the head of the firm's use of terse language, the hard pressure of ink on the page, and the way Mr. Ryan's letters neither slanted right nor left.

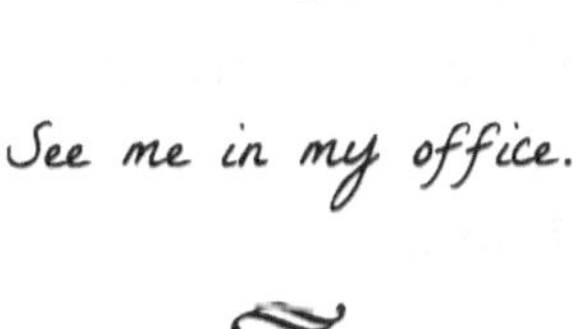

GRACE STARED at the words for only a beat, then stood, her hands sweaty and cold. A sure sign of rising anxiety that was annoying, but thankfully not that difficult to hide because she'd had plenty of practice over the years. A pep talk would help. Maggie could talk her off of the ledge if anyone could.

Grace reached inside her purse but came up short. She leaned back and groaned, picturing her cell phone laying on the passenger seat of her car, where she'd left it, still plugged into its charger. Without a phone, she wouldn't be able to dash into the women's room to call her sister.

Worse, her car battery would likely be dead by the end of the workday.

Grace slid another glance outside the window to the colorless day. She swallowed. If she hurried, she could zip downstairs to grab her phone and be back before Mr. Ryan expected to see her in his office.

By the time she reached her car, her palms had earned their sweat, only they were no longer cold. After retrieving her phone, she instructed Siri to call Maggie.

"Aren't you supposed to be working?" Her sister was not one to spare words.

"I'm here. Something's up. I can feel it. Help me calm down."

"You're going to have to give me more than that."

Grace blew out a breath, sending strands of her long blonde hair aloft. "Fine. I showed up here early, you know, to get a jump-start on the week—"

"Because you've been an early bird from birth, catching the worm and all that."

"Are you gonna listen?"

"Proceed."

"It's just that, strangely, no one else is around. It's Monday, and there are literally dozens of employees, yet I'm the only one here. Well, except for one of the bosses." Her eyes flitted about the half-empty underground parking lot. "At least I think I heard him in there."

"So you were calling me to make sure that everyone else wasn't, what—raptured into heaven?"

"Ha ha ha."

"I don't have time for this, Grace." Maggie's voice sped up like she was multitasking. "I'm sure you'll figure out a way to put a positive spin on whatever might—or might not—be going on at work. And then you'll have them following after you."

"There's more. The boss left a note on my desk."

"You mean ... what was her name again? Judith?"

She shook her head. "No, not the woman who hired me, the boss that sends the entire place running for the fire exit when he thunders down the hall. Chase Ryan." She paused. "He wants to see me."

"Maybe he just wants to compliment you on the exceptional job you've done your first week."

"Considering we've hardly met, I doubt it."

"Hm. Are your hands still clammy?"

Grace wiped her palms down the hip line of her skirt again. "I'm worried about what he's going to say about me taking a vacation so early into my new job."

Silence.

"You did tell the human resources department about your non-negotiable month off, right, Grace?" Suspicion rang in her sister's tone.

"Not exactly."

"Grace Holloway!"

Grace pressed her hand to her temple. She wasn't about to mention that her parents' attorney had called to remind her about the very same thing, nor the guilt that lingered after their conversation. "You don't understand, Mags. This was the only interview I received after literally more than a hundred job applications." She would never confess to her family just how high the tally of her college loans had grown. Each one of her siblings had busy lives and problems of their own. Why should they have to bear hers too?

"I get it," Maggie said, "I'm broke too, but we've been over this a hundred and eighty-seven times and you drew the short straw. Remember, you were the only one with free time when our family situation was all settled."

"I know, I know. I still don't understand why our parents put that weird stipulation in their will."

Her sister didn't answer right away. Finally, "You know as well as I do that there's no getting around it. We've tried. If we want to inherit Mom and Dad's beach house—the only thing they've left us—then we each must live there for one month and fix up the place on a budget. No exceptions."

Grace nodded. She pushed back the frustration her eccentric parents' final words had caused, along with the grief that still rose over their passing, and hurried across the parking lot to her office building.

A whimper caught her attention and she slowed. She stepped closer to the only thing nearby, a shopping cart with a paper bag nestled inside. She heard the whimper again. Something in the bag rustled, and hesitantly, she peered into it.

Her sister's voice called out. "Grace? Are you there?"

Two marble-shaped eyes looked back at her.

"Grace?"

She whipped her chin toward the phone. "Sorry, Maggie. Gotta go. Will call you later."

The whimper grew into a howl.

Grace threw her phone into her purse and hitched it over her shoulder so her hands could be free. "What are you doing in there, little one?" The puppy wiggled in her hand, his black fur soft, his eyes dewy.

Grace frowned. She glanced around the parking garage but didn't see anyone lurking about.

She brushed a look into the pup's questioning eyes. "Now what am I going to do with you?"

The puppy answered her by aggressively licking her fingers with its sandpaper tongue.

Grace flipped her chin upward in a *why me* stance but had already made up her mind, consequences or not. "C'mon, little guy," she said and tucked him into the over-sized bag hanging over her shoulder.

If she hurried, she could find a safe place for the animal, then show up in Mr. Ryan's office with no questions asked.

The building's glass front doors were open and she charged toward them. A shot of pain seared her forehead and nose, and her respect for cartoonists grew as stars began circling her head. Or so she thought.

Apparently, the building's doors weren't open—just clean—and she had run headlong into them. Shock devolved into questions, like why she didn't think things through thoroughly enough, and would it be weird to show up in the boss's office with an icepack on her face?

A husky voice cut through her self-loathing. "Are you all right?"

Chase Ryan. *Of course.* She hadn't seen him there, standing inside the lobby, watching her slapstick routine in real time.

She covered her face with her hand and nodded. "Yes, yes. I'm fine."

"Do you need a medic?"

She peered at him through open fingers. A medic? What

is this, the military? His eyes continued to focus on her, concern knotting his forehead. He was either genuinely concerned or thought she was an idiot.

"You're Grace."

She started to roll her eyes but stopped herself. Her older brother Jake used to tease her with the title. "Pass the butter, Your Grace" or "Answer the phone, Your Grace."

The purse of Chase's tempting lips startled her. So maybe he hadn't been kidding …

"You are our new hire, Grace, aren't you?"

"Uh, yes. Sorry. Yes, I am." The bag on her shoulder squirmed, and she cinched it closer to her, adding, "Mr. Ryan."

"Call me Chase." His eyes narrowed. "And if you do not require medical attention, meet me in my office in ten minutes when I return."

She lifted her hand in a salute but caught herself, leaving her hand to dangle in front of her like a robot stuck in a pose. What was wrong with her? She was a rule-follower, a head-down-in-the-books kind of woman, not some rebel against authority. But for some reason, her world had been disrupted today. Yeah, that was it … she'd been thrown off by her family lawyer's early morning call and just needed a minute to get back into her usual routine.

He hadn't moved.

She nodded. "Yes, I'll see you inside." But Chase continued to watch her longer than was comfortable, his gaze sliding to her bag. She kept her focus on him, ignoring the puppy's whine, though why she didn't just tell him what she'd found, she didn't know. Again, she was … off this morning.

He cleared his throat. "Your purse is in need of attention."

She bit her lip and began to pull the bag from her shoulder when he pointed. "Wet spot forming. Perhaps your lunch spilled."

Sure enough, a dark spot had formed on the fabric of her bag. She lifted her gaze to his. "You may be right."

He nodded once, clearly satisfied. "You have ten minutes to handle that."

CHASE STRODE into the parking area, his employee on his mind. What was her name again?

Grace. Right.

Though still green, he'd heard she was smart. Top of her class. Bright future. All of it.

Too bad he had to let her go.

Chase's jaw clicked as he moved across the pavement, his mind unusually disorganized. "Pull it together, Ryan," he muttered.

He couldn't fathom why Grace had shown up for work today. Unlike all the others. Although maybe she had plans to hold that fact over his head, to use it like some kind of negotiating tool. Now was not the time for him to let his armor down. If he'd learned anything in the last few hours —or, really, in his lifetime—a woman with an ax to grind wouldn't stop until the object of her wrath had been turned into a mere stump.

He pressed his lips together, his mouth forming a grim line. He had not spent any time with the firm's newest employee, but he'd noticed her, especially the way she clipped her way through the office, her chin up, an I'm-here-to-take-on-the-world expression on her face. She had tried to keep up that stance when he'd watched her slam into the entry doors back there. Despite her shock, she had looked him in the eye, a noble attempt to wow him with a certain defiance, but he wasn't buying it. She was nervous. Unsure.

Would have been a perfect new hire, someone who wouldn't shy away from tough clients and their complicated matters. If only his life hadn't changed so dramatically in the last twelve hours, he might have enjoyed the challenge of helping her sharpen the skills she'd acquired in law school.

Chase strode toward the parking booth at the entrance of the business complex that his father owned, intent on getting some answers. What did the attendant know about all that had transpired in his office? What had he seen? With each step his anger grew, his teeth clenching harder.

Kate Little had started as his paralegal, but after she passed the bar and quickly proved herself as a force in law, she became one of his top employees—and more than that.

He should have known that their union would be too good to be true. The blame landed squarely on him. Had he not learned as a child that relationships weren't meant to last? That, contrary to the news—and social media—men weren't always at fault when relationships fell apart?

Forget fuzzy Mother's Day ads, the truth was, women could be as ruthless as men were purported to be. He'd seen that firsthand in his most formidable years and had decided long ago to put his trust in himself alone.

Though Kate had, temporarily, changed his mind.

Today, however, she had proven him right the first time.

His mind wandered back to the expression on his new recruit's face ... on Grace's face. He hadn't been able to shake off the way she'd looked at him, a mix of distrust and ... hope? What was in her head and why did it matter?

He flicked away all thoughts of her and, instead, steeled himself while approaching the booth. He had to stay focused. Especially now with so much at stake. He had a business to save and couldn't waste another second trying to figure out why Grace Holloway's presence, today of all days, caused his thoughts to linger on her.

As it turned out, the parking booth attendant hadn't seen a thing. Chase wasn't sure he bought the man's indifference. The operation had been too clean, too ... sinister.

Then again, he wasn't all that sure about anything these days. If only ... if only he had someone to talk through all this headache with, like he had once done with his cases. His father, until recently, had been his sole confidant, be it business decisions, matter handling ... relationships.

What might it have been like to have a mother to bounce things off of too?

That stray thought tumbled through his gut. He lengthened his stride, shaking off such signs of weakness and turning instead toward the tasks in front of him. Mainly, returning to his office to meet again with his newest employee—and cutting her loose.

So much for a quick dash out to her car. Grace shut her office door and hurried over to her credenza where she kept cans of tuna, water, and extra clothing in anticipation of long, lawyerly days of work. Carefully, she put her purse down and lifted out the tiny pup, who snuffled and wiggled in her grasp.

Grace frowned. How old was he? What could he eat—the tuna, maybe? Or wasn't he ready for solid food? She blew out a breath. She needed to get the little one to a vet soon, but not yet. She poured some water into a bowl and watched him lap it up. While petting his back, she said, "Sorry, friend, but you're going to have to stay here for a little longer."

Grace made a bed out of a sweater she'd kept inside the drawer. "Guess I won't be wearing this anymore." She laid the doggy on the homemade bed, holding her breath that he would stay still enough for her to traipse off to her meeting with Mr. Ryan.

She needn't have worried. He yelped once, then collapsed into a perfect circle. Before she'd had a chance to take a second breath, he was snoring.

She grinned. *Must've tired the poor little guy out ...*

The sound of footsteps brought her back to reality. No sense in putting this meeting off any longer. She hastily dashed a note to Mick, wondering when he would appear, and left it on his desk.

Puppy in my credenza. Don't ask. Please don't shut the drawer all the way. Will explain later.

She hadn't remembered the hallway being this *long*. This walk felt like a journey to the principal's office, not that she'd ever taken one herself. But she imagined it would feel much like this did right now. What did he want to talk to her about? Did it have something to do with the fact that she was the only one who'd shown up on this dreary day?

Light shone from the open doorway to Chase's office, and her unease grew with each step. She glanced around. Darkness prevailed throughout the sea of cubicles that fanned out in the large office. A frown tugged at her. Truly no one had shown up for work this morning? It's not like today was a holiday,

Well, even if it were she would have come in anyway, eager to build her presence here at the firm, to bill more hours, and if she were being brutally honest—to get out of the deep debt she had found herself in.

Just the thought of that mess made her heart beat faster, and not in a good way. She'd always been the careful one, the daughter who used spreadsheets, even in middle school. How she had managed to let her bank account sink as far as she had ... well, it would do no good to rehash the whys. Now she just needed to focus on the hows.

And one of the *hows* was keeping this job. She'd made a plan and intended to stick to it, even if her plans did sometimes feel like a shaky tower of cards. As long as no rogue wind suddenly blew in to topple said cards, she'd be fine.

Grace raised her hand to knock on the door frame but froze. Chase was bent over his desk, his hands rolled into fists, supporting him. He lifted his chin and looked her over, his jaw set, those watery green eyes of his intense. When she had encountered him down in the lobby, she'd thought how they reminded her of a fresh pool of water at the base of an unrelenting waterfall.

But not now. Now the green in his eyes had turned grey and steely.

He straightened, never taking that hard gaze from her face. "You chose to stay."

"If you mean that I showed up to work on what appears to be a holiday for everyone else, then I suppose you're right." She paused. "I have a lot of work on my desk right now."

She didn't mention that her duties also included copying

files to send to a client, summarizing records, and possibly even a run to the post office. Not exactly the tasks that she planned on doing forever, and certainly not the skills that warranted the hefty law school debt she had accumulated.

Chase walked around to the front of his desk, one hand shoved into his pocket. He eyed her, his expression a mixture of wariness and curiosity—maybe even a little distrust thrown in. Definitely some Mr. Darcy-at-the-ball vibes happening there.

"You really have no idea what happened around here."

His question was more of a statement, as if testing her. She licked her lips and let her eyes do a brief survey of the room. An electric pencil sharpener lay upside down at the base of one scarred wall. The quiet began to reveal other things she had not noticed earlier. The click of a clock. The whir of air-conditioning. The lack of printers printing and keyboards clacking, of phone calls being made and coffee brewing.

She swallowed. "Was it ... did something ... happen?"

He clenched his jaw, heightening the effect of his angular cheekbones. "Have a seat, Grace."

Silently, Chase walked to his high-back office chair and sat, resting his palm on the armrests. He fixed his gaze on her. "Kate Little has left the firm and she's taken most of the staff with her. And half the files. The good half."

Grace gasped. A dozen thoughts elbowed their way into her mind. "How-how do you know?"

He lifted a file and dropped it with a *thwack*. "It's all in there. She came in yesterday, apparently, and stole half of everything. Even the staplers."

"But ... why?" Grace couldn't fathom anything so ... nasty. She settled her gaze on Chase. Despite his impeccable choice of suit wear and the hard set of his chin and brow, a glint of something softer reflected in his eyes. Sorrow, perhaps? She felt sure he was trying to hide it, but he was keeping up the tough-guy charade with her anyway.

"I'm surprised you didn't already know about it."

A sinking weight settled into her stomach. She wasn't surprised, not at all. Grace had been trying to land a job in law for months, and with virtually no experience, she'd hit block wall after block wall. Then suddenly the clouds parted and Judith, the office manager, who had apparently gone with Kate, had given her a shot.

And now she knew why. It was as if employing her and leaving her behind was a parting shot at Chase, as if to say, "Here's some help for you—good luck."

She had no idea what Chase had done to tick off his lead attorney, but she hated being used. Hated it.

Seething, Grace lifted her chin. "What are we going to do about all this?"

One of Chase's well-formed brows shot up as if she'd startled him with her question. "I'm going to be speaking with my attorneys." He paused. "And ... I have to let you go."

2

G race blinked, sure she had not heard Chase correctly. Perhaps this was some kind of initiation rite. That had to be it.

He continued. "I have put in a call to my office manager ... and, well, she hasn't returned it yet." He sighed, picked up the file, and tossed it to the other side of his desk. "She'd know what kind of exit paperwork you'll need."

"Exit paperwork?"

"For unemployment."

She would *not* walk out of here unemployed. She couldn't! The word wasn't part of her vocabulary. While others in her class seemed to have some kind of financial lifeline, Grace had worked all through law school and even while studying for the bar. She didn't give up easily.

"I'd like to discuss—"

Chase's phone rang. "Excuse me. I have to take this."

On any other day, Grace would have taken that as a cue to step away and give the boss some privacy. But today wasn't like any she had ever experienced, and she knew if she left, she'd be out. So she stayed, holding onto hope that with a little convincing, she could change Chase's mind.

Still, she tried not to appear to be listening to what was beginning to sound ... personal.

Chase drummed his fingers on the desk, his gaze pointed toward the ceiling. "Does he need to go to the hospital?" He was quiet a moment. "Uh-huh. I see. Good."

Even as Grace contemplated what her next steps would be, she found herself leaning into Chase's change in tone.

A small grin broke out on Chase's face, surprising her. "No, I've not eaten today." He nodded, still listening. "Yes, ma'am. I will." He paused, his expression softening, as well as his voice. "Thank you for the call, Amelia. I appreciate it."

When he clicked off, she wished she had followed her original instinct and left the office. What if he counted voyeurism against her? Before she could muster an apology, Chase stood, lines etching his forehead. "I'm hungry," he said. "You?"

She opened her mouth but shut it again, confused. Food was far from her mind. Did he not just fire her? *What the heck ...*

He walked around to the front of the desk and leaned his chiseled frame against it. "I know your lunch is ruined." He raked a hand across his hair, stress lines marring his forehead. "Let's go have breakfast. I'll explain more then."

"My lunch?"

He creased his brow further, a distinct vertical line appearing between them. "That spill in your purse from earlier."

Of course. The puppy.

She nodded quickly, wishing he hadn't remembered that

—let alone her graceful entrance into the building. "Right. Yes. You're right."

"So ... brunch?"

She eyed him. No light in his gaze. In a way, he reminded her of a puppy himself, one that had just been rapped with a rolled-up newspaper. "I need to go to my office first and take care of some things."

He nodded. "I will meet you in five minutes."

She dashed out of there, half annoyed and the other half downright curious. What in the world had Chase done to drive out so much of his staff? Grace laughed aloud, though it was anything but merry.

"What're you laughing at?"

Mick Smythe was squatting on the floor next to the credenza. Quickly, she shut the door behind her.

"You're here!"

Mick blew a raspberry. "'Course I am. You didn't think I wasn't going to show up my second week on the job, did you?" He paused and pointed to the open drawer. "Who's our friend?"

Grace shook her head. "Not now." She glanced at the closed office door while hitching her purse over her shoulder, thankful that the spot wasn't too noticeable. And it didn't smell. At least she thought it didn't.

"You okay?"

"Kind of." Was it her place to tell him what was going on? Especially since she hoped to change the boss's mind? "Listen, Chas—Mr. Ryan—has asked me to meet him for breakfast to discuss a few things. Can you take care of the puppy until I get back?"

Mick pushed up his glasses and shrugged, a comical smile on his face. "Sure. But can I just say something?"

Grace let out an exaggerated sigh. "Of course."

"Be careful. That guy's reputation with women isn't sterling." He paused. "I wouldn't let my sisters date him."

Grace fought a second urge to roll her eyes today. "Got it. Thanks." If he knew that she was about to try to save both of their jobs, he might have kept his thoughts to himself.

At the scowl she undoubtedly gave him, Mick raised both palms. "Just sayin'."

She unhooked the crossbody strap from her purse and handed it to Mick. He leaned his head to the side.

"To use as a leash. Better take her out to pee."

Mick raised an eyebrow and turned his gaze to the open drawer. He laughed. "Too late for that."

She continued to hold out the makeshift leash to him. "Please?"

He sighed and took the strap for him. "Fine, but you owe me."

If she saved both of their jobs, that debt'll be paid—and then some.

CHASE'S PHONE PINGED. Judith, his office manager, had sent him a text. Finally.

> Judith: You rang?

> Him: I would expect this from the others, but you?

> Judith: What can I say? I'm weighing my options.

He pressed his eyes shut. Weighing her options? Judith

had been with him, well, she'd been with the firm since before Chase had gone to college. She'd worked for his father, had encouraged him to go to law school, to study hard, and had stayed on after he had passed the bar and added his name next to his father's.

Judith Jones had more or less been his ear recently as things with his father became more ... precarious.

Chase's eyes opened and he blew out a harsh, pent-up breath, the taste of rejection like poison. He glanced at the door to Grace's office as it opened and she stepped into the hall. He second-guessed his decision to invite her to brunch on today of all terrible days, but he knew he'd leveled a blow to her fledgling career. The invitation felt like a penance of sorts. For exactly what, he wasn't sure. Or maybe the invitation was one very big avoidance tactic.

All he knew was that those perky eyes of hers dulled at his layoff announcement. And though he doubted she was different from every other ladder-climbing woman he'd had the misfortune to meet, that sad look she'd given him had prodded him into doing something he was not known to do: let her down easy.

GRACE SAT ACROSS FROM CHASE, wiping her hands on a napkin repeatedly, unwilling to accept his explanation. He'd made mention of a falling out between him and Kate, but there had to be more than a lovers' spat at the core of this sudden exodus from the Law Offices of Ryan & Ryan.

But what?

He turned his chin slightly, eyeing her. "I will email you a letter of recommendation."

Yes, well, that'll pay the bills ...

Chase's phone rang and he scowled. She was beginning to wonder if that phone ever slowed. He snapped a look at her. "Sorry. Need to take this." He lifted the phone to his ear. "Judith."

Grace sipped her coffee, her interest perked at the name of the firm's office manager on the line. The woman spoke loud enough for the neighboring table to hear her—not that she was complaining.

"I got your texts!"

"I assume you have weighed your options, then," Chase was saying in response.

"For heaven's sake, Chase, you didn't think I was serious when I texted you that!?"

Chase's brows rose. "Then what did you mean?"

"Honestly, I had no idea Kate had this planned. I had a dentist appointment this morning—didn't you remember that?"

His shoulders visibly relaxed and he shut his eyes for the briefest moment, his humanity coming through. He sucked in his top lip. "No. Your personal life had not occurred to me."

"Don't get snippy with me, Chase! You need me right now, I must say. What are you going to do with the cruise this weekend? Have you thought about that?"

Grace peered at him over her coffee mug and caught him sneaking a look at her. No doubt he was wondering how much she had heard. She had no thought of feigning ignorance.

"Chase? Your father is expecting you—and you cannot NOT show up there. And you'd better not show up alone either."

Chase snapped another look at Grace and scowled. He

turned back to the phone. "Listen, I'm speaking to Grace right now. Why don't we continue this later."

"We definitely will. I will see you as soon as this novocaine wears off. I hate this stuff."

He slid his phone back into his pocket, a tiny smile emerging on his face.

"Happy to learn that your office manager hasn't jumped ship?"

His eyebrows knit together. "Something like that."

She set her mug down. "So, speaking of ships, a cruise this weekend. Mexico?"

He lowered his brows. "Yes."

"Hmm."

"What does that mean?"

She shrugged. "Timing seems ... rough."

He set his jaw, his look like a dagger. "It's an obligation."

She laughed. "Really? Sounds like a vacation to me."

Those green eyes of his darkened to the color of a dense forest. "I'm not in the habit of discussing my plans with my employees."

"Perfect. I'm not an employee anymore."

"Do you always say what you're thinking?"

She paused, knowing this could be a trick. One of her law professors always said, "Know when to stop talking." She did not want her boss—well, her potentially ex-boss—to think she could not follow this basic courtroom advice. "I like to think of it as saying what I believe, of not backing down from that."

"And you believe that I have no business taking a vacation at this crucial time."

She paused. "So what did Judith mean? She sounded almost shrill about, you know, your cruise and all."

He leveled a gaze on her. "She meant that I am obligated to attend."

"Bummer."

His mouth dropped open. "Are you ... are you laughing at me?"

"All I can say is I wish someone would obligate me to sail away on vacation."

"It's not as simple as that."

"Three days of no phone, maid service, all the food you can eat and champagne you can drink ..."

"And all the clients I can schmooze."

"Oh. I see. So that's what she meant when she said you'd better not show up there alone."

"Not exactly." He paused. "Your hearing is excellent, by the way."

"Then what exactly did she mean?"

"You are exasperating."

Her brother might have said the same thing to her a time or two. Grace did not respond to Chase, but instead leveled her gaze on him. Surprised by a jolt, she mentally swatted away all thoughts of wanting to kiss those frowning lips.

Chase sat back. "She meant that I'd better show up with a fiancée—and that I have until Friday to find one."

SHE WAS GOOD. He'd never known a freshly baptized lawyer to hold a poker face so well. Usually, that skill took time and practice.

Grace continued to stare at him, that impish look in her eye.

"Don't look at me like that," he said.

"How am I looking at you?"

"Like you have it all figured out."

She rustled a bit then. It appeared that she was biting the inside of her cheek. "I wouldn't say that, but some things are becoming clearer to me."

He sighed. "Like?"

She shrugged. "Kate was more than your co-worker; she was obviously your fiancée. You and she had a falling out and now she's trying to teach you a lesson."

"Is that right?"

"Well, it's a theory. Though ..."

"Yes?"

She wrinkled her nose. "I don't understand the part about having to find a fiancée by Friday. Seems rather draconian."

Chase crossed his arms. "Let me clear some things up for you: Kate was never actually my fiancée. She was pretending to be. For my father's sake."

"What?"

"Sorry if that doesn't strike you as particularly kosher, but we had an arrangement, which, if she had not broken it so spectacularly, would have benefitted us both greatly."

"Because you were going to what? Extend that pretend engagement into a fake wedding? And then break up with her?"

"You're onto me."

Grace exhaled. "Well, no wonder she's peeved."

"What's that supposed to mean?"

She leaned her head to one side as if assessing him. "Did you have it in writing?"

He narrowed his eyes at her.

She laughed a little. "So ... your ex-girlfriend, the woman

you worked with day in and day out, had promised to be your 'fiancée'"—she made quote marks in the air as she said it—"but you didn't have anything in writing mentioning that this was all make-believe." Grace shook her head. "Men."

"I'm confused."

"I'll say." She shifted in her chair, turning to face him dead on. "She didn't want it to be fake."

Why was he discussing this with her? Chase shook his head. "No, you've got it all wrong." He stuck two fingers into that space between the buttoned collar of his shirt and his neck, loosening his tie as he did. "She-she—of course, she knew it was fake!"

Grace stared back at him and Chase admitted to himself that he'd never met anyone quite like her. Any other office newbie would be sitting in silence across from him, perhaps nodding her head on occasion, definitely agreeing with him —at least outwardly. But she told him what she thought— exactly what she thought—and didn't appear to be on her way to some kind of nervous breakdown as she did.

Then again, he did just fire her.

Tension crept up his back. "Fine. Look. I get that you're wondering about my predicament and your imagination has run amok."

Grace picked up her mug of coffee and took a slow sip before saying, "Not really."

Chase's brow rose. He could barely conceal a crack of a smile. "You really are teasing me now."

She shrugged. "Maybe."

"Well then, will you allow me to explain?"

She set the mug down rather quickly, he thought, then flashed him a look. "Please do."

"My father, Timothy Ryan, started this firm, and though

he has long since retired, he has certain requirements regarding its future." Chase swallowed, thinking. "They are rather old-fashioned, but he's my father and I aim to honor his request."

"To have a fake fiancée?"

He speared her with a look, ignoring the clench forming in his jaw. "Bottom line is that Kate had agreed to do the honors, but now that she's run off—"

"With part of your firm."

He leaned in. "Now that she's gone, I need a replacement."

Grace's eyes widened briefly, then settled. Finally, she spoke. "That was some job requirement."

"It was never a job requirement. If it had been, I'd be in jail." He shook his head. "No. She and I were close at one time and she knew my father, so she agreed to play along. That's all."

"And then she changed her mind, spread the word that you were a cad, and almost nobody showed up for work. Well, other than Mick and me."

Chase sat back. "He showed? I wasn't aware. Guess not everyone fell for her story."

"Not all of us knew about it." She batted the air as if she was moving on. "Have you tried calling her?"

Was she serious? He narrowed his eyes. "Of course I did." He shook his head. "Kate and I had a tumultuous relationship. She started at the firm as a paralegal. When she passed the bar, I kept her on and gave her a new title."

"Girlfriend?"

He scowled. "Attorney-at-law."

"Yes, of course."

"We were a good team, as colleagues. I think we both

realized early on that anything more between us wouldn't work. In the meantime, my father had become more insistent that my"—he cleared his throat—"reputation change. Do you understand?"

She nodded, a somber expression overtaking her features. He hated the effect.

"The stories aren't true, you know," Chase finally said.

"None of them?"

His gaze turned steely—he could feel the hard change of it, but couldn't seem to control himself. Part of him wanted to throw cash on the table and end this now. The other part? He took a breath, steadying himself. The other part of him wanted to lunge across the table and kiss away that pout on her lovely face.

But that would only serve to brand his so-called reputation into her mind.

Chase forced himself to pull his gaze away from her. He had to take back control of this conversation. "As I noted earlier," he said, benignly, "Judith will be in soon to talk to you about applying for benefits. I will have her speak with Mick as well."

"That won't be necessary, at least not for me."

A knife-like piercing shot through his shoulder, accentuating the rising tension within him. She wasn't going away easily. "Oh no?"

She was leaning forward now, determination etched into her expression. "I have a proposal for you. A business proposal."

That one brow of his that tended to shoot up at moments when his interest was piqued just did its thing. "Really. And what exactly would that be?"

"I need a job—and you need a fiancée." She looked him square in the eye. "Consider the position filled."

SO IT WASN'T EXACTLY the job she had envisioned? Without her quick thinking, Grace would be standing in line at the unemployment office. And she would also be sitting in front of her computer for hours each day, submitting her resume to cold and ruthless human resources bots. At least now she could pay her rent. And maybe eat.

She may not be working as a lawyer at the moment, but she'd shown herself as resourceful. That was something, right?

"Something's not stacking up," Mick had said while cleaning his glasses on the tail of his shirt. "You're outta here, but I somehow kept my job."

She shrugged, not meeting his eyes. The puppy yelped for attention and Grace was happy to pick him up for a cuddle.

Mick moved closer. "Why aren't you ticked?"

"Because, frankly, I have a lot going on in my family right now anyway." By the time she talked Chase Ryan into giving her back her job—which is precisely what she planned to do after this little weekend was over—she'd make sure to negotiate a month off to fulfill the requirements of her parents' will. Ha!

Mick gawked at her. "You and the boss looked pretty cozy when you came back."

She frowned. "Really? I can't imagine why you'd say that."

Mick stared at her a beat longer than was comfortable

before breaking eye contact. He put his glasses back onto his nose and strode toward the door. "Guess I better go. Judith said she wanted to talk to me about some things." He paused and turned to snare her with a look. "You going to be okay?"

"I'm perfect. Don't worry. I'm glad you didn't get tossed out of here." He didn't have to know that she threw in Mick's job as a condition of her agreement to play Chase's fiancée. Nor that she and Chase agreed it would look better if she wasn't actually an employee of the firm during this little charade.

"Well, then, good luck." He hesitated before leaving the office, holding the door with one hand. "Grace?"

"Yes?"

"I meant what I said earlier."

"Which was?"

He blew out a breath, as if exasperated. "That I wouldn't want that guy dating my sisters." He turned and left without waiting for a reply.

Grace rolled her eyes at the back of her office door. Mick did not understand just how close they both were to getting the ax, and really, this outcome, strange as it was, turned out perfectly. She neither cared to date Chase nor marry him. Shoot, the thought of marrying anyone before her career gained traction was as attractive as men in three-quarter-length pants.

Best of all, she and Chase were strangers to each other, so there was no chance of any kind of romance. Though she may have been too busy to keep up with gossip surrounding her "fiancé," she had learned enough in the past few hours to know that she would never—ever—allow herself to give a playboy anything as complicated as her heart.

3

———

If Grace did not fully understand the gravity of her financial situation, she may have thought she was living a fairy tale. She knew her way around the shoe department of her favorite mall. And on occasion, she liked to splurge on a Michael Kors bag.

But this.

This ... dress.

She turned around, arching slightly to view the low lunge of the dress's back in her stateroom mirror, its satiny cream fabric hugging her waist. Swoon! Who knew that an eighty-year-old's birthday party would require such formal wear?

The past few days had sped by with too many errands to count. She'd shopped for cruise wear, both formal and not—thankfully on Chase's dime. She had also packed, found a neighbor to take care of her puppy—yes, she'd kept the little guy—and met Chase to pick up a marriage license.

That last errand gave her pause.

"Why do we need that if it's a fake relationship?" she'd asked Chase.

"You don't know my father." He'd looked at her almost grimly. "The man's a stickler. Always has been. I want to have it should he challenge us in some way. It'll expire in ninety days."

A recurring thought pecked away at her thoughts. Though marriage had been far from her mind over the past few years, when she did picture what that sort of thing might look like in her life, one thought won out: a church wedding to a man of faith, like her father.

Grace brushed away that niggling thought for the umpteenth time. She took another peek at herself in the mirror. They'd checked into the suite as a "happy" couple and then promptly retreated to their corners. Hers had a window to the outside that she gazed out of liberally, and with her door closed to the other end of the suite, she might as well have been alone.

Grace sighed, stepped into her silver slides, and picked up her shimmery clutch. She pushed aside reminders of her life at home, with its growing piles of bills and uncertain future, including her parents' suffocating requirements regarding their Last Will and Testament. She rehearsed what she'd been told about the night ahead and waited for Chase to let her know when it would be time to go.

The knock on her door caused her to catch her breath. "It's showtime," she whispered.

Slowly, the door opened and Chase peeked in. The smile on his face froze, his gaze sliding down the length of her.

Grace turned to look at the mirror and then back to Chase. "Is everything all right? Is this dress okay?"

He closed his mouth and the lines in his forehead flattened out. He stepped inside. "Yes, of course. The dress is ... beautiful."

She pushed out a sigh and laughed. "Well, get in here then. You had me worried."

He stepped inside, his posture stiff. She took in the shine of his black tux. He'd chosen to wear a black shirt instead of the customary white. "You're staring," he said.

"Not really." She shrugged. "Ready to go?"

He pursed his lips in a way that she was beginning to interpret as *unsure but plowing through anyway*. He offered her his arm. "I am. Let's go."

As they entered the ballroom, a blast of cool air lifted tendrils of hair off of her shoulders. Golden lights illuminated the stairway and she gasped. So beautiful. She tightened her grip on the crook of Chase's arm as he led her down the grand staircase and into the ballroom. A sea of finely dressed guests parted, admiring them with a smile. She caught more than one nod gently sent Chase's way.

The age of the crowd leaned heavily in the octogenarian range, though plenty of thirty- and forty-somethings did their best to balance things out. Chase had explained that the room would mostly be attended by other lawyers, a judge or two, and some longtime clients. Not many family members would be in attendance.

Chase stopped. She glanced at him, noting a sudden falter of a smile. She followed his line of vision to a slightly stooped, white-haired man rising from a table abutting the dance floor. A woman in a flowing seafoam-green dress stood next to him, beaming.

Chase brushed her hand with his fingers, gently took it,

and guided her toward the elderly gentleman with a sparkle in his eyes.

"Grace, I'd like you to meet our guest of honor. This is my father, Timothy Ryan."

The man took Grace's hand and kissed it. "You are even more beautiful than my son told me."

"Happy birthday, Mr. Ryan."

He continued to hold her hand, his gaze holding hers. "Please, call me Dad."

She stilled. Grace had been floating, swept away by the beautiful clothing and impressive venue, the azure seas, and the promise of obligations met for the foreseeable future. It had not occurred to her that her fairy tale might actually be someone else's real life—and that she would soon take part in dismantling their ... role-playing.

Chase cleared his throat, startling her.

She smiled at Chase's father. "I hope you enjoy every minute of your celebration, Dad."

Lights flashed. Photographers abounded inside, the lights from their cameras causing snippets of the crowd to ebb and flow in her sight. She'd prided herself on her studies, but an uncomfortable sense settled in her stomach. Chase's father was well-known, apparently, and she had been caught unaware.

That girl ... always with her head in a book!

Lift your chin every once in a while, so you don't miss out on life!

There are book smarts and life smarts—make sure you have some of both!

The admonishments she'd heard most of her life rose in her mind like a faceless monster and a knot formed in her stomach. She'd walked in here, ready to play a part, but at what cost?

Timothy pulled his son close and whispered something in his ear. Chase watched her the entire time his father spoke, his brows reflecting a flittering of different emotions.

"What is it?" Grace asked.

Chase did not answer her at first. A dour look settled on his face, but then he quickly erased it. He offered her his arm as if that flit of emotion hadn't happened. "He would like us to dance."

She nodded. "I would love to. That is, of course, if you know how."

He shrank back, both brows raised. But then ... a sparkle emerged. "I did not spend all those years in cotillion for nothing."

"The fox-trot it is."

He laughed now and the heartiness of it buoyed her temporarily. Chase led her to the dance floor. He cupped her left shoulder blade and pulled her closer. The formality of it all made her want to giggle, but she followed his lead. She'd attended enough weddings in her lifetime to play along. She could even do the chicken dance if it were suddenly called for.

They moved around the dance floor, stiffly, making small talk. Pleasantries. Meaningless conversation. More than once Grace caught Chase's gaze darting around the room.

"How do you think it's going so far?" she asked.

He blinked and caught her with a look. "Sorry?"

"Your father seems pleased."

He swallowed, his Adam's apple rebounding. "Yes, yes, he does."

His gaze traveled elsewhere again.

"Anything I should know about?"

He whipped his gaze back to hers. "Pardon?"

"Your mind is somewhere else, which is fine, of course. But if there's something I should be aware of, I hope you'll share it with me."

Chase wrinkled that space between his eyes again, pouring his attention back on her more fully now. "Does that mind of yours ever stop?"

"Sadly, no. Makes sleep difficult."

He smirked but continued to watch her. They were eye to eye now, neither gaze wavering. Goosebumps alighted on her skin and she shivered slightly.

"Cold?" He didn't wait for her to answer, but instead loosened his stance and pulled her even closer. The warmth of his touch on her bare arms caused a flutter of something unexpected within her.

Chase leaned close, his lips grazing her ear. "Peter Mayer is approaching us. He may cut in."

She shrank back. "The toy magnate?"

Chase nodded, pressing his lips together as he kept his gaze focused somewhere over her shoulder. "Educational toys. Our biggest client and one that I intend to keep—despite the shakeup."

Must be one of the important clients he'd mentioned. Maybe even *the* most important client ...

A man's voice broke her concentration. "Chase, may I dance with your beautiful date?"

"Peter! Great to see you. I'd like you to meet Grace Holloway." He glanced at her, his eyes pleading. "Grace, Peter Mayer is the CEO of Mayer's Educational Toys and Games."

Chase let go of her and delivered her into the arms of another man. Like chattel.

She bit back a scowl and turned to Peter, lifting her hand. "It's a pleasure, Mr. Mayer."

He grinned widely. "Please, it's Peter." To his credit, he lifted both arms in a wide embrace but didn't touch her. "May I?"

As they twirled around the floor, Peter said, "You are a miracle worker, I hear. I was so pleased to learn of your engagement to Chase." He leaned closer. "You really have saved the day."

She quirked her head to the side. "You are kind to say so, but I don't believe my presence is any sort of miracle."

"Oh but it is!" He shook his head, a sad smile on his face. "Poor Timothy is getting slower these days. Well, many of us are, I'd say. But he has been my representation for many years—you do know that we create hundreds of family-friendly education products, don't you?"

She didn't, but she also did not let on. "Toys and games, yes."

He smiled. "It has always been my contention that we are represented by the finest individuals, whether it be accountants, public relations, and, of course, attorneys."

"How lovely that Ryan & Ryan has represented your interests so well for so long."

"Hm. Yes." He cleared his throat. "You must know that Kate Little has been in touch with my office."

Alarm raised the peach fuzz on her neck. She steadied her expression. "I'm sure there were some loose ends she intended to sew up."

He chuckled. "You are diplomatic. As I mentioned, poor ol' Timothy has essentially turned the reins over to your

Chase, and I was beginning to wonder how long our partnership could last."

She frowned. "I don't understand."

Both of his eyes widened. "I am not a judgmental man, but Chase's reputation as a ladies' man—I am putting that politely—well, that is not exactly the sort of collaboration that we are most comfortable with putting forward."

"I see."

He smiled kindly. "Forgive me. Where are my manners? Of course, this point is moot now because I can see that you have tamed Chase's wild ways. You know, there is nothing like marriage and family to change a person's stripes, eh?"

A trickle of sweat dripped down Grace's back. She longed for a glass of water to stem her body's slowly rising temperature. Her parents, imperfect as they were, taught her that love and respect for each other, and for God, were utmost. Every time she attempted to think otherwise, her thoughts boomeranged right back to the example they'd left her and her siblings. What would they think of her predicament now?

She kept the smile on her face, though grief attempted to yank it away. "Will you excuse me?" she said, finally, letting go of Peter's hand. "Thank you for the dance."

"You are most welcome."

She turned, glad that she was able to get away before her hands did that slimy thing they liked to do when stress reared its despicable head. With her eyes on the prize of the ladies' restroom, Grace darted forward, but a hand at her elbow stopped her.

"Hello, beautiful."

She spun around at the sound of Timothy's voice. "Hello, Dad."

The elderly man blinked and frowned. "Dad?"

Grace reached for his hand, a slight laugh in her voice. "Maybe you were kidding when you asked me to call you that."

He licked his lips, nodding, his eyes seemingly unfocused. He leaned forward. "Who are you?"

She knit her brows together. "I'm Grace—Chase's, uh, fiancée."

Timothy's face split into a wide smile and he began to pump her hand. "That is exceptional news! Oh my, yes, spectacular news!"

Chase approached. "Dad? Grace?"

Timothy turned around. "Hello, Chris! I was just enjoying your lady here."

"Chase?" Grace said.

Timothy put his palm onto his temple. "Chase—not Chris. I am sorry, Son." He exhaled robustly. "All this frivolity has my mind in a scramble."

Chase put an arm around his father. "Why don't you and I go have a seat at the table." He turned his chin to Grace. "It looks like you were headed to, uh ..."

"The ladies' room."

"Right. Well, find us when you return. I believe they are about to serve dinner."

Grace nodded at Chase and squeezed Timothy's wrist. "I'll be back momentarily."

Inside the restroom, she turned on the cold water spigot at the sink and allowed her hands to cool, her thoughts a jumble. First Mick, then Peter Mayer had specifically warned her about Chase's bad boy past. Now Timothy didn't seem to recall that she and his son were together at all.

Probably too much of a rare occurrence in his eyes ...

Not that it mattered to her all that much. This weekend would be over soon enough and she would no longer need to pretend to be marrying Chase. At least not publicly. Sure, the engagement would have to continue for a time, but other than this cruise, Grace had not made any other commitments to appear as anyone other than herself.

The scent of White Shoulders wafted beneath her nostrils. The woman who had been standing next to Timothy when she'd first met him stepped up to the sink and smiled at Grace in the mirror. "Oh, it's you!" she said.

"Hello again," Grace said. "I apologize for not introducing myself earlier. I'm Grace."

The woman's rose-tinged cheeks shone. "I know exactly who you are, dear. You have made quite the impression already."

Grace's cheeks grew warm. "That's kind of you to say." She glanced at the woman's left hand and noted the absence of a ring. Chase had clammed up when she'd asked about his mother, saying only that she would not be in attendance. She surmised that the woman was Timothy's date, though it would have been nice to be sure about that before she said anything.

The woman towel-dried her hands. "Well, you enjoy yourself, you hear?"

"Thank you. I plan to do just that." She hesitated.

The woman slowed, her expression puzzled. "Did you want to say something, dear?"

"I didn't get your name."

"My name is Amelia."

"That's beautiful." Grace dried her hand on one of the supple towels in a box on the sink. "Well, I hope you and Timothy enjoy yourselves."

Amelia chuckled. "We will if he follows my instructions!"

Grace smiled. "Have you been together a long time?"

The woman gasped a little. "Oh, my, yes. But you don't think we're lovers now, do you?"

She would not have put it that way, no. "I didn't mean to pry," Grace said. "You are his date, though, right?"

Amelia's smile turned slightly sad. "I guess you could say that—I am his caregiver."

"Oh."

She nodded, knowingly. "You aren't aware of Mr. Ryan's condition."

"I, uh, no. I only met him tonight."

Amelia nodded. She cleaned wet spots off the sink with her used towel and discarded it into the waste can. "I probably shouldn't have said anything. Please don't mention to Chase that I overstepped—you won't, will you?"

Grace shook her head, a few tendrils of hair brushing her shoulders. "Consider my mouth closed."

Amelia smiled at her appraisingly and began to step away, but stopped. "You really are a welcome addition to the family."

Grace stayed behind as Amelia walked out of the restroom. Secrets, it seemed, were the underlying theme of this grand shindig, but how could she not agree to keep Amelia's when she was carrying around one of her own?

GRACE TOOK A SEAT BESIDE CHASE, her mind far from the rule of law. She barely noticed the din of the crowd, her mind tethered instead to her newfound knowledge of Timothy's condition. Her heart wept at the thought, the reality too close for comfort. Her own mother had experienced a similar decline, though Grace had been too wrapped up in her studies to realize it.

And then it was too late.

Chase leaned toward her. "I took the liberty of ordering you a glass of white wine, but if you would prefer something else, I'll see to it."

"This is perfect." She took the glass from him, grateful for the distraction, momentary as it might be. She lifted the glass, giving him a "cheers" in the air.

Chase peered at her, his eyes turning dark as a forest. "You okay?"

She took another sip of wine. "Are you aware that Kate has been in touch with Peter about his business?"

His jaw hardened. "He said that?"

"Yes. If it helps." Grace had successfully steered the conversation away from her deepest thoughts and back toward a topic she might be able to do something about. "He seemed satisfied that you had, um, changed your bad boy ways."

"Glad to know it." Chase sat quietly, digesting the news.

Then, as if she hadn't said a thing, he pushed away from the table and draped his napkin on the back of a chair. Grace watched as he stepped up to the band and borrowed a microphone. She fervently hoped he wasn't planning to call out his top client in public.

When the music fell away, he began to speak. "As many of you know, I'm Chase Ryan, and I'd like to welcome you all today. My father is a friend to many, but he's always just been Dad to me." He paused.

Was that emotion tugging at the corners of Chase's mouth?

His voice faltered. "If you would all raise your glasses, I'd like to lead us in a toast." Chase pressed his lips together for a moment, allowing his gaze to sweep across the room before landing on his father. "To Timothy Ryan, the smartest, most noble, bad-ass lawyer on this earth. You're my hero. Happy Birthday!" He raised his glass to a chorus of "hear hears" followed by thunderous applause.

A full-of-heart speech was the last thing Grace had expected from Chase, who, up until today, had seemed quite comfortable in his tough-as-granite wrapping. She turned her chin slightly, letting her gaze take him in. His eyes greeted hers, lit by that mixture of emotion she had noticed, and perhaps something a little fierier, too. She turned away when a server set a lavish plate of food in front of her.

They dined on the most exquisite lobster and filet mignon that Grace had feasted on, probably ever. The butter alone would stay in her memory forever. It wasn't that her family lacked anything growing up, but her parents weren't keen on indulging much of their hard-earned money on high-brow food. To that end, her mother tended a large garden no matter where they lived, and she used it to feed her brood vegetarian meals until well into their teen years.

She bit back a smile at the memory. Her brother, Jake, would often sneak in cardboard boxes of burgers and fries from In 'n' Out for her and her sisters after their parents had gone to bed. Too bad she and her siblings had not hung onto their camaraderie once they became adults.

"You seem lost in thought," Chase said, breaking her concentration. His voice had a less formal tone to it now as if this family affair had broken down a wall or two. Or a curtain at least. "What's on your mind?"

She swallowed a bite of food and shrugged. "Thinking about my family, my siblings ... parents."

He paused, as if weighing her words, then spoke quietly enough that only the two of them could hear. "Where are they all now?"

"My brother Jake is an architect not too far from LA—though I hardly ever seen him, Maggie's a hairdresser in Arizona, Bella's a librarian in Washington, and Lacy works in sales at a hotel in Vegas."

"Wow. Big family. Are you originally from Los Angeles?"

"Not really."

His forehead bunched.

She paused, thinking. "We lived all over the place but spent a lot of summers just a couple hours up the coast from here. Never really wanted to go too far away as the others did."

"And your parents?"

Grace swallowed before answering. "They died last year. Car accident."

Her hand was resting on the table next to her plate and Chase reached over, taking it in his own, his brows knitting together in unabashed sympathy.

She shrugged it off. "It's okay. Sad, but okay. We are all doing ... fine." That was as close to the truth as Grace was willing to go.

He squeezed her hand tighter. "I'm sorry."

Their eyes caught as she offered him a shy smile in gratitude, his hand lingering on hers until a commotion next to her drew them away.

A gasp.

The distinct clamor of silver against china.

A groan.

Timothy had slumped in his chair and began to slide to the floor, but Amelia fell to her knees and caught him in time.

"Dad!"

Chase lunged from his seat, with Grace close behind, and took over for Amelia, cradling his father in his arms as he gently lowered him to the floor.

Amelia looked up at Grace, her layered dress splayed all around her. "I'm stuck. Help me?" Grace offered the woman her hand, but it was a struggle. "My knees aren't so good anymore," Amelia cried.

A dark-haired woman in a chiffon gown knelt on the floor next to Chase and his father. "I'm a doctor. Please let me have a look."

Grace pulled her phone from her handbag, intending to call for help, but Amelia stopped her with a touch. The caregiver wheezed beside her. "Won't help here, dear. We're out to sea, remember?"

She dropped her phone back into her bag and bit her lip, watching the doctor assess Timothy. Thankfully, she could see the rise and fall of his chest. His eyes appeared to be open slightly.

A man in a pinstripe suit arrived, his expression sobering. He joined the others on the floor and held Timothy's head as the elderly man struggled to get words out.

"He's a doctor, too," Amelia whispered. "Offered to give me something to keep Timothy calm, but I turned him down. Maybe I should have listened."

Grace patted Amelia's shoulder, attempting to calm the woman. "You trusted your instincts and that's what a caregiver needs to do. That's all anyone can ask."

Amelia's eyes were rimmed with red. "It's just he's already on too much medication, in my opinion ..."

Timothy moved then, looking agitated, and Grace didn't know whether to glance away or stay close in case her help was needed. Not that she had a clue how she could assist in such a serious situation. For the time being, she stayed rooted, if anything, as a support to Amelia.

Chase leaned in toward his father, who was trying to say something. "What, Dad? What is it?" He pulled back and hesitated. Then he turned and looked up at Grace, confusion etched across his face. "My father would like to speak to you."

Fear caught in her throat. "Me?" She attempted to wick away the perspiration forming on her hands by wiping them on a napkin.

Chase's eyes bored into hers. "Please."

Quickly, Grace knelt on the floor, vaguely aware of the crowd making a ring around the group of people cobbled together to help the ailing honoree.

The male doctor instructed her to slip her hand behind Timothy's neck. "Like this," he said. She did as she was told, achingly aware of the lack of color in the old man's face.

"I'm worried about you," she squeaked out, peering into his eyes.

"You are a good woman."

Emotion caught in her throat, but she swallowed it away. "What is it you'd like to say to me, Dad?"

"I'm dying."

She shook her head. "Oh no, no. You aren't dying. I think you just need some rest—it's been a big weekend for you."

He reached a hand to her face and touched her cheek, his eyes unwavering. "Marry my son before I die."

"I—"

"Promise me." Those same eyes, flooded with unshed tears, implored her.

This was no longer a game. To Timothy Ryan, it had never been. Was this what life was like for her mother in those last days? Was she confused about what was real—and what was not?

"Please," he whispered.

She couldn't save the past, couldn't revisit her mother's difficulties and offer some kind of help. Oh, how she wished she could. Instead, as Timothy continued to hold her gaze, weak as it may be, she found herself nodding and trying to keep herself from shaking uncontrollably. "Yes, of course, I will." Suddenly everything about this business arrangement felt wrong. Stupid. Shameful. And she longed to make it right.

A man appeared with a wheelchair. The female doctor in the gorgeous gown leaned in. "Miss, if you'll step back now, I would like to bring Timothy to the ship's medical center for observation."

"Absolutely."

Chase and the doctors helped Timothy into the chair. "It's all right, Dad. You're going to be fine," Chase was saying.

Timothy raised his hand into the air and Grace grasped it. "Tomorrow," he said.

She leaned her head closer to his mouth so she could hear him better. "Tomorrow?"

Timothy nodded weakly, but a tiny smile had found his mouth. "Marry my son tomorrow. On board."

Grace watched the entourage wheel the guest of honor away, all the while wondering what in the world she had just agreed to—and how she could possibly back out now.

"DEARLY BELOVED ..."

A man couldn't look like Chase—angular jaw, unyielding dark eyes, delicate crow's feet that contradicted his serious persona—and not garner attention. If she were to stare too long, she too could become caught up in his movie star looks. There. She said it.

Grace had been purposely avoiding the fact that the man she had come here with, the man she had a fake relationship with, well, there was a reason that *this* man could have the kind of reputation that he supposedly had.

She had ignored all those warning signs for reasons of self-preservation. She needed work and had seized the low-hanging job when it dropped in front of her. Only she hadn't been prepared for how quickly things would turn ...

Judge Cape cleared his throat. He stared at her, his brows oddly close to hitting his hairline. "Are you ready to repeat after me now?" he asked.

She startled. "I'm sorry?"

He nodded. "Repeat after me ..."

Her parents were devout people. They loved God and family and tradition, even if they had always been strangely untraditional in many ways. How many times had they moved and rented out their house, for instance? And what was with her dad's obsession with lone backpacking? He'd be gone for weeks, and when asked when Dad would return, her mom would only shrug. And whistle. She whistled a lot while puttering around their home—be it an apartment in the city, a cabin in a wooded area of the foothills, or the beach house that they frequented during school breaks.

Oh! If they were to see her now, standing before a judge

on this cruise, marrying a man she hardly knew, well, she couldn't imagine. At least it wasn't a captain marrying them. What a cliché that would have been!

"Did you understand the question?"

The judge had said something. What was it? Chase was watching her, his eyes smaller than she remembered. Or maybe he was blinded by the sun.

Grace could have said no, she *should* have said absolutely not, but last night after the drama had died, Chase had told her the depth of Kate's deception ....

"My father was grieved by my reputation—or my perceived reputation," Chase had said. "He blamed himself. He wanted to teach me a lesson ... by not allowing me a partnership in the firm—until I found a wife. He put it in his will!

"Kate had agreed to play my fiancée. She suggested we begin building a clientele all our own, and like a fool, I agreed. Now, most of those clients are gone. Not only that, she's been courting my father's clients as well. I only wish I knew why they seem to be choosing her over me ..."

Anger welled within her. "Why can't your father just change his will?"

The weight of grief marred Chase's features, his eyelids heavy, his gaze imploring. And suddenly she knew. The pit of her stomach filled with a weight all its own.

She touched the crook of his arm. "I understand. Your father is showing signs of dementia."

Chase blinked rapidly. He'd seemed so stern, so enigmatic when she'd first met him, but he was flesh and blood—in a fine suit.

"I'd hoped ..." His voice trailed off, but he didn't have to say a thing.

"You'd hoped that the party would prove that he was okay," she said, "that he had the presence of mind to correct his will before it was too late."

He nodded.

She pulled her hand from his arm and ran it through her disheveled updo, additional strands of pinned hair falling to her shoulders. Grace sighed. "Only now those signs of his illness have been made clear to everyone on board."

Chase pressed his lips together, his eyes desolate. He reached out for her. "I promise I'll get you out of this. Until then ..."

As his words died away, she became resolute. "Until then, we had a deal."

His gaze hardened slightly. "That's not what I meant."

She lifted her chin, meeting his eyes with her own. "But you were going to ask me if I would go through with the wedding, weren't you?"

His eyes bored into hers. "Yes."

"Grace?"

Now as they stood in front of the judge with cruise ship guests all around them, Grace looked into Chase's eyes again. His father's eyes. Timothy sat in a wheelchair to the right of his son, his skin sallow, waiting for her to answer the judge's question.

Her own father had begun to look that way after many months of caring for her mother who had not been well. None of her siblings had any idea how long their mother had been in that state—nor the toll it had been taking on their father. She regretted that. And at this moment, her next move felt a bit like penance.

Judge Cape asked her another question, and before she knew it, she said, "I do."

Quickly, Chase followed suit.

And then the cameras began to flash.

4

———————

She had been ignoring her phone for days. When the ringing stopped, the pinging of incoming texts began.

The first text she received was from her sister, Maggie. "You're married?! What in the world …!"

The next was from her sister, Lacy. "I figured you'd be the first one. Thanks for the invite."

Then one from her sister, Bella. "Married on a cruise. Sigh. How romantic! When do we meet him?"

The last one scared her the most. It was from her brother, Jake. She hadn't heard from him in months—none of her other siblings had either. At least she now knew he wasn't dead. "He'd better be worthy of you."

A knock on the door of Grace's apartment startled her, though she had been expecting him. She opened it to find Chase standing on the other side. He pressed his lips together, a lift to his brows, and waited.

She rolled her eyes and turned her back toward him.

Two suitcases and an insulated bag of groceries sat neatly on the floor next to her coffee table.

Chase rustled behind her, his voice cutting through the tension. "Ready to go?"

She peeked over her shoulder. He hovered at the threshold of her apartment, his sandy hair closely cropped, the tan skin of his neck framed by the open collar of his deep-blue dress shirt. He watched Grace with an understated smile, his laugh lines belying an emotion contrary to the dread she felt.

Then again, he wasn't about to take her to his family's beach home for a month where he'd likely face demons from his past *and* have to explain her presence to his family.

Stupid reporter.

In the days since Grace had married Chase Ryan in the middle of the Pacific Ocean, she'd had to hide behind dark sunglasses and a nondescript baseball cap more than once. She'd been too caught up in the moment to remember the photographer and reporter who had been on board to cover Tim's birthday.

Turned out that, in addition to the grand birthday ball, he'd scored a couple of bonus stories, namely, Tim collapsing at his own party and the wedding of his playboy son.

The calls and texts she received the day after they had disembarked told her all she needed to know: Her secret marriage was not so secret anymore. A front-page mention in the newspaper took care of that. Everyone aware of Chase Ryan suddenly also knew *her*. The news had reached her family too, even as far and wide as they had flung themselves.

She nodded at Chase, and he approached her bags. He

gestured toward them. "Is this it?"

A whine split the silence, the same funny sound the puppy had made when she'd hidden him in her bag at the office on the first morning that she and Chase officially met.

Chase's eyebrow darted upward again and he quirked his head at her.

Grace blew out an exaggerated breath. Technically, she wasn't allowed to have an animal in her apartment, but what was she supposed to do? Put the poor little guy out? She'd put up messages on Facebook and Nextdoor and had called the animal shelter, but no one had claimed the puppy, whom she had affectionately named Zeke—short for Ezekiel. Nothing against animal shelters, but she couldn't bear it.

As it turned out, her sweet pup had become more of a savior to her than she was to him. She felt sure of that.

Chase touched her arm and she tried not to flinch. He nodded toward her bedroom door. "May I?"

She waved her hand in a way that said *whatever* and watched him enter her sanctuary. Soon, he'd be stepping into her childhood second home, the one that her family had run away to whenever life in the city became too much to handle, the rambling home on a slight rise above the sea that she and her siblings refused to lose to some charity. Not if she could help it.

Still, she had a love-hate relationship with that house, which might seem rather unbelievable considering its location. Realtors had called her parents for years with buyers ready to snap it up, problems and all. One Realtor in particular—someone named Lillian—was a particular nuisance. But her parents would never even consider any offers.

When they died suddenly, she figured that the beach house, along with her parents' other worldly possessions, would have been left to their children. Imagine their surprise when they learned that their parents, after giving most of their money away to charity, had nothing but the paid-in-full beach house left.

And that if she and her siblings failed to follow some specific rules, the house would be given away too.

Chase reappeared with the pup in his arms, its soft black fur dusting his skin. She pushed off her foreboding thoughts about the house and tried to focus on the moment in front of her.

Chase winked at her. "Guess our family's growing quickly," he said.

He was trying. She knew it. But the bottom line remained the same: Grace had married Chase, a man she barely knew. *Married* him. Grace glanced at Chase standing there looking all hot and adorable with Zeke simpering in his arms. He could be on a calendar or something. He'd been born with a playboy's face and grew into a man with a body to match. Who was she to think that he'd ever change? Or want to?

"Are you okay?" he asked.

She steeled herself. Another thing she knew? She would never, ever fall in love with Chase Ryan. Ever!

"Fine," she said. "Let's go."

They took off for the coast minutes after piling her luggage and Zeke's crate into Chase's Range Rover. Grace glanced out the window at the changing scenery, noting that nothing at all looked the same anymore.

CHASE HAD BEEN DRIVING for more than an hour without so much as five words from his passenger. And the words she did say were limited to one- and two-word answers.

"Would you like to stop for coffee?"

"No."

"Any particular choice of music you'd like for the ride?"

"Not really."

In some ways, this would have been easier if she were his employee instead of his ... wife. He would be able to fire her for insubordination, for example. Or for all-around surliness.

She gasped a little, catching his attention. But when Chase turned to her, she kept her eyes on her iPad screen. She'd been staring at that blasted screen for most of the ride, except for the couple of times she turned to coo at Zeke.

"Big project you're working on there," he said.

"Hm."

"It's a long drive. Anything you want to bounce off me?"

She turned, her face heart-shaped, her soft-brown eyes taking him in. In a word, lovely. Even so, would he have noticed her had their paths not passed in such an extraordinary way? He dared to wonder.

She wrinkled her expressive brows at him. "Do you need directions?"

He frowned. "No, that's not what I meant."

She stared at him for another beat, nodded, then went back to her work. Or whatever it was on that screen in front of her that had kept her occupied for most of the ride. For all he knew, she was creating a recipe list for their month at the beach house.

Sexist pig.

Even he winced at his thoughts and the likely rebuke he'd have received should he have voiced them aloud.

Chase fumbled with his phone, found the music app that

connected to his stereo, and clicked it once. Ed Sheeran was singing a ballad. Big surprise. He reached out to turn off the stereo, but Grace's hand stopped him.

"I like that," she said.

Their gazes collided and he was silenced, the vague sound of wheels on the road rushing past in his ears. She dropped her touch from his wrist, the moment gone, and he put both hands back on the steering wheel in the ten and two. Or should it be nine and three? Or eight and four?

He scowled. Since when had he wasted time contemplating trivial matters? Chase slid another glance at Grace's iPad. She appeared to be working over a spreadsheet like she had an eye affixed on the bottom line.

Just like Kate.

And his mother.

And when the numbers did not line up the way they wanted? Poof. Gone.

Chase swallowed, a trickle of heat climbing up his neck, darkening his thoughts to match the coming night. Grace had seemed all too ready to propose a deal when she had learned about his predicament. A financial proposal. Isn't that what all the women in his life ever wanted?

A phone call he'd taken from Kate two days ago ate at his insides.

"You *married* her?" she had said instead of hello, her voice more shrill than usual. She was the queen of drama—a pastime of sorts for her— but he had always been on the same side of her derision.

Not so now.

"Something ... something about this is not stacking up," she'd continued.

He pictured her, sculpted dark brows drawn together like

knitting needles on a rush order, her red lips quirked upward at one corner, that low hum she made when she was thinking.

It occurred to him that this wasn't over in her mind. He would have to be cognizant of that.

He pushed away thoughts of his ex and her vengeful ways and concentrated on the scenery through the windshield. Swaths of crimson and gold burned through the darkening sky. They were close to the coast now, all indications pointing to "a sailor's delight" of a day tomorrow. At least he had that to look forward to.

Grace's sigh reached him over the music. He slid another glance at her, but she continued to stare at that spreadsheet, working her teeth over her bottom lip the entire time.

Normally he would have appreciated the silence. Far different from the inner workings of a busy law office with its non-stop calls and interruptions. He should be relieved, and when he stopped licking his wounds long enough, he realized he was.

Though she had married him in a noble gesture toward his ailing father, Grace Holloway had given Chase no indication that she had set her sights on anything else where he was concerned. She'd even signed a prenup without hesitation.

As the sky turned to black and the woman next to him continued to focus elsewhere, Chase knew he'd made the right decision to take Grace up on her proposal—detour and all. The last thing he needed was a woman to fall for him— or worse yet—fall for his money. Whatever was left of it. He needed to protect himself from that happening again, and from the looks of it, he had.

5

———————

The first thing she noted about the beach house was the smell, a familiar mix of salt, sand, and damp wood. And the sound of wind tunneling its way between gaps of warping windows. Grace stepped inside and stopped, grief hitting her in the windpipe. That was a brand new memory that came with the place.

"What is it?"

Chase's smooth voice provided an instant of comfort, followed by one of dread. Her parents hadn't been in this house in, what, months? Yet their fingerprints were all over the place.

Though she longed to spin around and bury her stinging eyes in the hollow place at the base of Chase's neck, Grace pulled herself together. She inhaled sharply and forced herself to look around the great room that had hosted not only her family but renters for ages.

In the dining area, an old map hung over the scarred wooden table, a faded testament to her and her siblings' nightly geography lesson.

The couch and her father's old chair were upholstered in deep grey with threads of black, perfect for hiding hot dog grease and other evidence of food eaten in the living room.

She took several more steps inside. Oak-stained cabinets bore dark smudges from years of touch. Although no dishes were present, a metal colander sat atop the dish drainer, as if waiting to assist in producing a meal. Next to it, a spray of fresh daisies sprang from an old tumbler.

She plucked the note from among the flowers:

Welcome home, chickadee! Love, Wren

Their longtime neighbor must have received word that Grace would be the first to come home.

Chase's hand on her upper back brought her to the present. Softly, he said, "Would you like to take Zeke while I grab the luggage?"

Grace nodded. She dropped the note on the counter and took the pup from Chase's arms. They'd made a pitstop about a half hour before to let the little guy roam on a grassy area, so she held him close and burrowed her fingers in the folds of his skin. She wound her way through the hollowness of the old house, stroking Zeke's fur over and over again, cooing to him as she did.

She stopped on the threshold of her parents' first bedroom—the original master bedroom of the place. Frayed drapes that were once the color of fresh tangerines hung from painted metal rods hiding the fact that a showstopper of a view lay just beyond the now-beige coverings and wavy glass windows.

Chase appeared beside her. "I'll put your things in here."

She shook her head. Even though a bedroom and bath had been added many years ago, and her parents had moved upstairs to use that one, somehow this one still reminded her of them.

"No, it's yours," she said. She couldn't stay there, not now. "I'll take the room down the hall."

He nodded once. "Lead the way."

She led him to a room with a double bed against the wall and draped with a beige bedspread with a big blue whale in the center of it. The walls of the room had been painted in sea glass green, as had the nearby wicker bookshelf and TV stand. A huge overstuffed whale sat on the floor in a corner. The windows were much smaller than the ones in the other bedroom, but they had been replaced after an incident involving a flying block of surf wax.

She'd have to give Jake a hard time about that ... if she ever saw her hard-headed brother again.

Chase put her suitcases on the floor, beneath a window. He looked at her with that one eyebrow stuck in the up position.

She stared back at him.

"Guess I'll get to bed."

She nodded. Worries over her tragic financial situation had dulled in comparison to the flood of memories that washed over her as she stood in this whimsical room that hadn't changed much over the years. That and the fact that she had brought a fake husband home with her had pretty much eclipsed all other thoughts.

"Grace?"

She allowed her eyes to fully focus on Chase. His dark eyes seemed to drink her in, and though she shuddered at being caught bare with unresolved concerns, she couldn't look away. *In another place, at another time ...*

He smiled. "Sleep well."

"Good night," she said.

Chase dipped his chin, eyes locked on hers, and backed out of the room, closing the door behind him as he did.

GRACE OPENED HER EYES, her phone a harsh wake-up call. "Hello?"

"Good thing you answered," Maggie said. "Did I wake up your Mr. Charming?"

Reflexively, Grace turned her head to the empty pillow beside her. She exhaled and shut her eyes again. "Hold on a second."

Grace swung her feet to the ground and padded across the room to grab her jacket, which she slipped on over the yoga pants and T-shirt she'd slept in. She grabbed a beanie from her suitcase and pulled it low over her ears.

Her sister's voice floated through the phone's speaker. "I don't have all day."

"Hold on," Grace muttered into the phone. "I'm going outside."

Grace stuck her head out into the hall and looked around. The aroma of fresh coffee met her senses, but otherwise, there was no sign of Chase. Or Zeke, for that matter. She made a quick exit through the side door at the end of the hall, past the room she and her siblings and friends once gathered in to watch TV ad nauseam.

Outside, clouds had gathered to greet the morning sun rising in the east. She stopped. Her mother's pink bench stared back at her, paint fading, but otherwise, strong enough to hold her. She licked her lips, unable to fully see that bench without her mother sitting on it, her chin lifted toward the sun.

"Grace?"

She scowled, pulled her coat around her tighter, and plopped down on her mother's bench. "Okay. I'm here."

"We want to meet him."

Grace licked her lips and glanced out to sea. She knew this was coming. It was the reason she had asked Chase to join her here for her month-long stay. She couldn't let the truth come out, not after the charade she'd agreed to had gone as far as it had. If her siblings knew the truth, they'd spill it. Then where would they be?

She watched a gull land on the sand next to another one and nudge it away. The first gull nudged back. "When will you be here?"

Maggie laughed. "That's not happening. We'll do it by video call tomorrow night. I'm guessing you have your computer with you, am I right?"

"I do."

"Well, since you didn't exactly invite us to your wedding, I'm sure you don't want us on your honeymoon either."

Grace shook her head. "It's not—"

"Whatever," Maggie interrupted. "I'll call in and you and lover boy should plan to get cozy around the screen. Family meeting at 7 p.m. your time."

Maggie hung up before Grace could say goodbye. She grimaced at her phone, wanting to pitch it at those bickering seagulls.

"Good morning." Chase had appeared at the bottom of the worn, wooden staircase that led to the sand. Zeke tried to scamper up the bottom step but got stuck and began to whimper. Then he lifted one tiny leg and peed on the corner of the first step.

Grace scrunched up her face, a smile breaking out. How could it not?

"C'mere, little guy." Chase scooped up the dog, and Grace tried not to notice his bicep flex. He plopped Zeke into Grace's lap and stood back as the puppy practically mauled her, his sandpapery tongue greeting every exposed inch of her, which was, basically, her face.

Grace laughed. "Silly, silly, puppy!" Fur and paws and happy snorts burrowed themselves into her neck.

Chase stood a few steps down looking scruffy and wearing the kind of smile she'd seen before, the kind that transformed weekenders from work-weary travelers to beachcombers without a care in the world.

Chase's arms were crossed as he watched her cuddling with the puppy. "I made some coffee."

She nodded.

"Left you plenty."

"Thank you. I had to, uh, take a call."

He quirked his head.

Did she want to mention just now that her siblings wanted a meeting with both of them?

"So," she said, "you're a morning person, then."

He let out a slow laugh and dropped his arms to his sides. "We have to be in our business. Clients expect that."

She shrugged. "But you could have slept in today."

His eyes snagged her with a look. "I suppose I could have had someone not been begging for my attention."

Grace squinted down at him from her perch, warmth rushing through her. Then Zeke snorted and stretched his enormously long tongue to give her one swift lick on the chin.

She laughed. "Ah, I see. Sorry about that. I'll make sure to get up early tomorrow and walk him."

Chase shrugged and edged closer to her, taking two steps up. "Wasn't a problem." He glanced out to the cresting sea then swung a look back to her. "Tell you what—we can switch off. One of us makes coffee while the other walks the dog in the morning."

"Good idea. Like partners on a project."

"Sure. Like partners."

Grace stood with Zeke tucked into one hand. She'd be lying if she said she didn't care to linger there on these steps, but she'd read some troubling emails on the drive out. Sure, Chase was handsome—hot, really—and he liked dogs, which was a plus. Zeke snuffled into her hand as if to agree.

But if the emails Mick had forwarded to her were true, she had already taken on more than she had anticipated.

"Well, hello there!" Wren appeared near the base of the steps. She wore a yellow sun hat tied at the chin over her black curly hair and a smile as wide as the sea. "Saw the lights go on last night but didn't want to disturb you."

Grace scrambled down the stairs. "Wren." She hugged the woman, drawing in the faint scent of burnt cedar.

Wren pulled back slightly and allowed her gaze to sweep across Grace's face. "You are a sight, dear one. How I've missed the Holloways around here." There was a hitch in her voice.

The lines in her face had deepened and strands of grey invaded the hair framing her face. But otherwise, she hadn't changed since Grace had last seen her. She appeared to be the same woman who would show up on a whim to chat about nothing and everything with her mother during those lazy summers when Grace was a kid.

"Wren, I'd like you to meet … Chase." She faltered on the introduction, knowing she should have said "my husband."

Wren clutched Chase by the elbows and looked up into his face as if memorizing him. "I heard the news. You're a strapping one, aren't you?" She laughed and it was so familiar that the sound of it made Grace, once again, miss her mother.

"A pleasure, Wren," Chase said.

Still smiling, Wren stood back, looking from Chase to Grace. "Now, I know you are newlyweds and all, but I hope you'll stop in for some lavender lemonade soon." She reached over to Grace's hand and gave it a squeeze. "I would love to catch up and get to know your man over here a little better. Will you promise me?"

A part of her didn't care to ever promise anything again. How would she handle the questions about how she and Chase met? About their engagement? She couldn't tell her mom's old friend the truth, but the thought of lying made her stomach twist uncomfortably.

Grace nodded. Of course, she couldn't say no to Wren. Then she reached over and pulled the woman into a hug. "I can't wait."

CHASE POURED himself another cup of coffee, eager to tackle more email before day's end. He had been making progress with Peter Mayer, who, even with his father's health hanging in the balance between life and confusion, continued to take his calls. He surmised that, although Kate was surely trying to lure him to her new firm, Chase's marriage to Grace had hopefully altered his ex's plan.

Despite it being Saturday and the lure of the expansive beach out there, he had work to accomplish for the toy mogul. Part of that was doing whatever he could to keep Peter's business for good.

Chase took a seat at the marked-up wooden dining table. He and Grace had settled into the beach house like an old married couple, sans the personal history. He'd made simple ham sandwiches for lunch and she'd accepted one from him. She had eaten hers at the butcher block island, while he'd taken his to this table that would serve as his office for the month.

As he dumped cream into his mug of coffee, he paused. Four plastic sandwich bags had been turned upside down on the sink drying rack. She cleaned out and saved plastic baggies? Odd.

His mind wandered back to their stops on their travels here. Though he had tried to buy her dinner, she'd refused. While he ordered a burger and a Coke, she'd opted for a side salad and water that she insisted on paying for herself. Later, when he'd ordered a latte at a coffee house, she'd asked the barista to refill her water bottle.

And what was up with all those coins she had emptied from her purse earlier in the day? He'd watched her methodically counting them out. Then she looked up at him and froze, her hand hovering over her stash, fingers dangling as if still counting ...

The screen door clamored to a close and Grace tumbled into the kitchen looking windblown and hurried, her rings of blonde hair in a tangle.

"Phew!"

"Cold out there?"

"What? No, not really." She glanced down at Zeke who skidded into the kitchen. "Got him out just in time, that's all."

He took in the mongrel that was currently searching nose to the ground for fallen morsels. Chase looked up. "Ah, I see."

"And I picked us up some muffin tops from a new bakery nearby." She held up a bag.

"Muffin tops? They're the best part."

She froze, a shy smile upturning her mouth. "That's what I said to the proprietor too."

"You'll have to take me to this bakery sometime."

She shrugged. "If you're nice to me, I will. Such a nice addition to our little beach town."

He clucked his tongue. "One way to show you how nice I can be is to let me help you with the pup next time."

She raised an eyebrow in a way that reminded him of himself. "You can help potty train a puppy?"

He shrugged. "Why not?"

She gave him a smile-frown, the kind that said, *I don't believe you but whatever* ... "He's almost there, I think. And let's be real—" she glanced around the great room—"it's not like he could hurt anything around here."

Chase crossed his arms, the mug of coffee in one hand. He leaned his backside against the tile counter that housed the sink's vintage faucet. "This place has good bones."

"You mean it's a dinosaur."

He laughed. "Naw. It's old, that's for sure, but it's solidly built."

"How can you tell?"

He gulped his coffee and set the mug on the counter.

"Because I didn't feel like it was going to be washed into the sea last night when the wind came up."

"So you're going the scientific route."

He grinned. "Never mock the gut feeling."

Something curious crossed her face then, as if she wanted to express a thought but suddenly caught it before it left her mouth. Chase pressed his lips together and waited, but when she didn't say anything, he continued. "You haven't told me much about why we're here, Grace."

"Oh but I did. I'm here to fulfill my part of the will's stipulation and you're here because of that busybody reporter on the ship. If he wouldn't have scooped our, um, event, then you'd be off the hook."

He pondered that. "I'm curious about something. You had only been working at the firm about a week when we had our ... meeting. Right?"

"Mm-hm."

"So had you already discussed this month-long vacation with Judith?"

"Is that a problem in your eyes?"

He raised both of his palms. "I'm not saying that. Was just curious."

She seemed to take a page from his book when she narrowed her eyes back at him.

But he couldn't seem to stop himself. "Because it would be rather unusual to approve a vacation this early into a person's tenure."

Silence. That shy smile had turned into something altogether different, her eyes tiny marbles. Finally, "You have got to be kidding me."

He huffed a laugh. "Hey, just thinking out loud."

"No, you're not. You're goading me on, trying to pin something devious on me."

He went still. Is that what she thought? Was she right ...?

"Maybe you ought to have ..."

He shifted. "What? Thought this whole thing out before dragging you into my life?"

The hardness of her gaze told him he'd hit the right button. He exhaled. Probably shouldn't say another word, but he was having a hard time keeping his thoughts to himself. "I just don't remember her mentioning it. That is all."

Grace slammed the dog's leash onto the counter. "Maybe you should keep your thoughts to yourself."

He coughed. "I am not accusing you of anything. Was just a simple question."

Grace's expression hardened and her chin jutted out, her eyes aflame. "Save that tone for the courtroom." Her voice was measured, firm. She seemed to swallow back her fire in the next breath as if realizing that this predicament wasn't going away. "We're in this together, you and me, for better or worse, and I won't be talked to like that."

Chase felt his chin tense. "Where is this coming from?"

She licked her lips and huffed out a breath, that fist still pounding into her side. "It's been a long week, Chase. Let's just get through this, all right?"

He stared at her, searching for some sign of why she'd suddenly turned from the happy-go-lucky woman with muffin tops in a bag to someone who clearly couldn't stand the sight of him. He gave up. "Whatever you say."

But she continued to stare at him. "My sister Maggie called today and the family wants to meet you."

"You didn't say anything to her about ..."

"Our arrangement? Of course not. I couldn't do that to ... to ..."

"Me?"

She looked at him like she wanted to gouge his eyes out. "To your father. Poor man believes all of this." She waved her hand dramatically toward him. "Anyway, we're being summoned to a meeting tomorrow night via video chat. It's going to be a weekly meeting to talk about the house and, well, whatever."

"And you'd like me to join you?"

She quirked her head to the side, her eyes like saucers. Sarcastic saucers, if there was such a thing. "Yes. That's why I said 'we're'."

"I can do that."

She allowed her arm to drop to her side, a look of resignation pulling down the corners of her mouth. Chase swallowed. The moment stood between them like the stereotypical elephant hogging up space. He wanted to reach out and touch her, to smooth away that smile, and draw her into an embrace, but would his intentions be misconstrued?

Likely.

So he stayed put. No need to carry on the charade outside of the public's eye. He'd meet her siblings tomorrow night and play his part to convince them that nothing was amiss in this sudden union with their sister. The women, he knew, he could convince. The brother might be tougher opposition to contend with, that is, if any of them actually opposed Grace's marriage. Had he even asked her about their reactions?

"Well, guess I better get this little guy fed." Her voice had softened slightly. She squatted down to pet Zeke, who had collapsed in a circular heap by her toes. "You hungry, buddy?"

Zeke raised his small head, then let it drop back down again. Chase squatted next to them and cupped his palm over the pup's head. He glanced at Grace, considering the variations of emotions he'd seen run across her face in the past few minutes. She'd come in breathless yet seemingly content. That had changed in a short time until she settled into what appeared to be resignation.

Though this was a business arrangement from the start, and she was being paid well for her part in it, Chase couldn't help the tug on his insides to make the entire month as tolerable as possible.

"Tell you what," he said. "I'll feed Zeke and take up walking duties tonight after I spend some time working."

"That's what I'd planned."

"Really." He pinned a look on her. "What about tossing a coin for the rotation?"

Grace stood up and stretched her lithe body side to side, a breathy sigh filling the quiet. "I already did," she finally said, "and you lost."

6

———

"Dad, it's good to hear your voice."

"It's good for me to hear it too." His father laughed in that old way of his, the sound of it comforting.

With his phone in his ear, Chase trudged through the sand, letting the leash out more until Zeke could test the temperature of seawater with his paws. Chase stopped and took in the setting sun over the shuddering waves. "Amelia says you are doing better than expected," he said. "I'm very glad to hear it."

"That woman is trying to kill me with her constant needling, always forcing me to eat, and to take poisons."

"Dad ..." Chase's voice held a warning.

"Enough about my, uh, health. How is ... how is the girl?"

Chase swallowed the lump in his throat. Did his father not remember Grace's name? Again? "You mean my wife." Even to his ears, the words were foreign-sounding, the feel of them strange on his tongue. "You remember her name, don't you?"

"Yes, yes. The woman."

"Whose name is …"

"Where are you anyway?" His father's voice turned surly. "I never see you anymore. When are you coming around?"

Chase frowned. Where had this neediness come from, this sudden change of mood? His father had always been the one with more appointments than room on his calendar, more visitors than quiet.

"Dad, let's try this again. You remember the cruise, yes?"

"Um. Yes."

"Good. And the woman who was with me. Pretty, blonde … kind smile. You remember her, too, right?"

"Um …"

"Think, Dad. She and I were married! Right in front of you!"

A pause followed by what sounded like the phone tumbling around inside a dryer. Finally, a guarded voice came on the line.

"Chase, it's Amelia."

"Where's my dad?"

"He is taking a rest."

He clicked his jaw, the sea no longer the comfort it had been, the sun now gone and darkness rolling in. "Put him back on a moment. I'd like to say goodnight."

"I'm not going to do that, dear."

Chase clenched his jaw. "Why not?"

Amelia continued, her voice gentle but firm. "It is very important that your father not become unduly stressed."

"He doesn't remember Grace's name. I was attempting to help him."

"By extracting it like you are taking a deposition? No, Chase. That is not helpful to your father. Remembering that you have a wife at all is an accomplishment at this stage."

"But ..."

"I must insist that you do not stress him. It will do no good, Chase. And it very well may do harm."

"I see."

Amelia's voice softened. "Chase? I want to say that it's a good thing you married Grace when you did. Your father is so pleased ... when he remembers it. I know this is something that he deeply wanted for you, even if he isn't as aware of it as we all would want."

Chase said goodbye to his father's nurse and shoved his phone back into the pocket of his windbreaker. Amelia didn't know about the arrangement Tim had made regarding passing the baton to him, a stipulation that still gnawed at him. He didn't feel much like walking anymore and it was a good thing—Zeke didn't either. The puppy had found a pile of discarded mussels to sniff and pee on, and then promptly collapsed beside them on wet sand, as if done for the night.

In one swift move, Chase lifted the puppy and carried him back to the house, cradling him. He left his sandy shoes by the door and stepped inside, the savory aromas of garlic and oregano greeting him. His stomach growled in response, and he wandered into the kitchen, his eyes slowly adjusting to the light.

Grace stood in front of the old, chef-grade stove, tending to a pot of something, the burnished light from the overhead fixture cascading down the messy bun she'd pulled her hair into. The light continued down along the long, slender trail of her shoulders. She hummed softly, her yoga pants rolled up, her feet bare.

He stopped, waiting, his whirring mind slowing to an

easy speed. The dog grew comfortably heavy in his arms, his slow and tiny breaths making damp spots on Chase's arm. He continued watching her, the moment like a gift just for him. Whatever it was that had gotten him so dusted up and riled minutes before had fluttered away on a tendril of heat wafting from the stove.

She turned abruptly, her eyes widening for an instant. She regarded him in a way he could not quite interpret.

"Well?" she finally said.

He took a step further. "Well ... what?"

She stirred the air with the wooden spoon in her hand as if conjuring up conversation. "Are you ready to eat?"

A slow grin stretched across his face. He couldn't have stopped smiling if he'd tried. He hadn't had a home-cooked meal in years. Living in one of the densest cities had provided him ample opportunity to dine on just about any kind of food one could imagine—most fare within walking distance of his condo. Chase had savored some of the best that the city had to offer.

But at the moment, not one of those dishes came to mind.

THE WAY CHASE dug into seconds of her spaghetti and meatballs, a person might think the man had never had a home-cooked meal in his life. Grace continued to watch him, not in a creepy way, but in between bites of noodles she allowed her gaze to take him in. Though he ate with gusto and flashed her a smile in between bites, something heavy lingered. She supposed it had to do with the predicament they'd found themselves in. Living a lie, but not able to correct it just yet—nor for the foreseeable future.

"You made this from scratch?" Chase said.

"I did."

That smile again and a slow wag of his head. "Best sauce I think I've ever had."

Goose bumps raised on her arms and she smiled into her bowl before raising her gaze back to his. "Really? It's pretty simple."

"Doesn't taste like it."

"I've been making this sauce since I was pretty little. All of my siblings learned. Just need to have the patience to slow-cook the tomatoes, blending them with oregano and other spices. Oh, and the wooden spoon is important."

"That why you were waving it at me when I walked in?"

She laughed. "Hazard of the sauce-making process. You have to stir the pot, scraping the sides regularly with a wooden spoon." Grace shrugged at him, keeping her expression sober. "Sorry, but it's true. No wooden spoon, no delicious sauce."

He raised a brow at her, but instead of appearing as some kind of chastisement, it looked almost comical up there. "Was your mother Italian?" he asked finally.

Grace breathed in slowly and exhaled. "She was and she shared her love of cooking with all of us." She didn't add that those ways, which centered on fresh food made at home for a fraction of the cost of meals out, were keeping her fed these days.

"Anyway," she continued, "I usually make large enough batches that I can freeze some. So I brought a jar with me."

"So that's the reason I didn't see you hovering in front of the stove for hours."

"Hey, somebody had to go buy the dog food."

He frowned, then followed her nod toward an enormous bag of dog food leaned up against the cabinet. "When did that get here?"

She leaned her head to the side. "I ran out and picked it up when you were asleep on the couch over there."

"I wasn't sleeping—I was resting my eyes."

"Oh, brother. All I can say is no amount of my huffing and puffing could wake you when I dragged that bad boy in here. Nor when I scrubbed years of dirt off of those old cabinets." She flung a wave toward the kitchen. "So I guess you were resting those eyes of yours pretty hard."

Chase wadded up his napkin and threw it onto the table —only it made hardly a sound. He tried to hide his laughter, but she could see it in the way those gentle crow's feet reached for his temples. "I might have dozed for a moment."

"Emphasis on 'might have'." She was laughing now too.

A grin broke out on his face and he glanced away as if thinking. When he swung his gaze back to her, he said, "We should probably talk about how we're going to approach the call with your siblings tomorrow."

Her laughter died on her lips. "Right."

"I take it you're not looking forward to it."

She shot him a look. "Would you be?"

"I've never had siblings in my life, but I would have to guess no."

"You've got that right." She exhaled, having lost her appetite. Grace pushed her plate away. "It's one thing to keep up the charade when texting, but I'm afraid they'll see the truth on my face."

Chase was quiet now. He rested his forearms on the table and leaned onto them. "Thank you."

She frowned. "For what?"

"For helping me save my business."

Grace would like to have taken credit, but the truth was, he'd saved her too. She'd been hired just in time, though even as she strode into work that morning of the uprising in the office, she had no idea how she would pay her rent. Or her student loans. If she were to strip away the variations of truth in all of this, she would confess that he saved her from going bankrupt. Or at least from going broke.

Not that she was suddenly rich. Years of scrimping had changed her, and though her bank account looked somewhat healthy at the moment, she knew how quickly things could change. She'd seen it in her own life. In her parents' lives, too.

Chase abruptly sat back. "I'll clean up."

Grace opened her mouth to protest, then stopped. Her mind wandered to an earlier time. Her father often lingered in the kitchen, snacking on leftovers, while her mother tidied up. Sometimes he would gently pull the kitchen towel from her hands and shoo her away, kissing her cheek before she went.

This night was not unlike that in many ways, and at this moment, she'd take what she could get.

7

"Hey, Slugger." Chase tossed a foam ball to Zeke, who lifted his head enough to see what had interrupted his nap. The doggy settled back down with a ripple sigh. "Seriously? You're going to leave me hanging here?"

Grace peeked over the island, more interested in the heart-to-heart going on between her dog and Chase than in the job search website on the screen in front of her. Not to mention the resume she was updating in a separate tab.

Some people curled up in rumpled sheets on Sunday mornings, but truthfully, she didn't have time for that. Not with the clock ticking on this relationship. So much for her plan to ask him to re-hire her after her fake fiancée bit had concluded. After this month at the beach was done, they'd surely be headed for an annulment.

Somehow she doubted he would ever make the mistake of running a law office with an ex again.

"Hey."

Grace looked up from the screen to find Chase looking

over his shoulder at her, a question in his eyes. "Zeke wants to know if you want to go on a walk with us."

She bit back a smile. "He does, does he?"

"He thinks it could ease the tension of tonight's video call if you give him some clues about what to expect."

"He said all that, huh?"

"He's quite the conversationalist."

She gave him a sad smile. "Unfortunately, I've got a load of things to do this morning."

Chase frowned. He glanced at Zeke. "Guess she's found something more important than you, buddy."

Zeke whined.

Chase speared her with a look. "You're breaking his heart."

Grace closed her computer screen, working to keep her expression neutral. "Fine. I guess a short walk won't take too long."

They slipped their shoes on while Zeke danced expectantly at their feet, his toenails adding character to the wooden floors. Grace pushed down the sense that an impromptu walk on the beach made them look like a "real" family. Would she ever find that kind of life?

Did she even want that?

Chase gave her a conciliatory smile. "You ready?"

"Sure thing."

A breeze had kicked up, making the balmy day more comfortable to walk around in. Chase began to walk south along the deep sand when Zeke had another idea and bolted to the west, nearly strangling himself.

"I think he's trying to tell you something," Grace said with a laugh.

"Yeah, he's trying to tell me he's in charge."

"Well, isn't he?"

Chase laughed, then shrugged. "Guess so."

Grace reached for Zeke's leash. "C'mon, I'll remind you about my siblings as we walk."

"Got it."

"Okay. Maggie's the oldest daughter. She's a single mom and works as a hairdresser, which is not surprising. She used to watch YouTube videos all the time about hairstyling and then practice on my sisters and me. Oh, and Jake sometimes. It got to the point where he would see her coming down the hall and take off running."

Chase laughed.

"Let's see. Then there's Lacy. She's sort of the middle kid and acts like it. Sarcastic as all get out. Likes to talk about how ignored she was, yada-yada-yada."

"I take it none of you apologized."

"Hardly." She grimaced and flashed him a look. "We probably made it even harder on her. But she's very success-ful, so I guess we could all take credit for that."

"How so?"

"I think she wanted to show us how wrong we were about her bossiness. Now she supervises a whole bunch of people in the hotel industry. Okay, moving on is me, and then my youngest sister Bella. She's quite bookish in that she loves books. Not ebooks, but real books, the kind that smell and can make you sneeze. You'll usually find her in an old bookstore somewhere."

"So she's like you."

Grace quirked a look up at him. He cleared his throat. "I noticed the books on your credenza. That's all."

Slowly, she nodded. "It's true. I love books, though I don't have the time for leisurely reading anymore. I guess"—she shrugged—"maybe she got that from me."

"Bella's the bookish one. Check."

"Oh, and she sells essential oils and never seems to let anything get to her."

He laughed, as if enjoying himself. "You haven't mentioned your brother."

"Right. Jake is ... complicated. He's the oldest."

"Hmm. He's going to want to kick my—"

Grace stopped. She looked over her shoulder. "What is it, puppy dog?"

The dog split the air with a bark and then began to dig furiously, wet sand flying behind him. She hadn't realized that she had, in essence, been dragging Zeke straight-legged across the sand.

"Must have found treasure," Chase said.

They walked back toward the dog, who kept yanking his head and barking presumably at his leash.

Chase squatted next to him. He patted Zeke's head and looked up at Grace. "I think he's trying to tell you something."

"Yeah, he wants off the leash, but no way. I've got too much to do. If I let him, he'll waste time here all day long."

Chase gave Zeke a conciliatory wink, then grinned at Grace. "Aw, c'mon, Mom. He just wants to be free to dig a little. It can't hurt for a few minutes."

Grace bit the inside of her cheek. She looked around. No other dogs in sight. "Fine. But you're in charge if he runs off after some birds."

Chase gave the dog another churning behind the ears. "Hear that, pup? Don't get me in trouble."

"Oh, there you are!"

Grace turned to find Wren behind her, her cheeks reddened from the sun, or possibly from being out of breath.

"Were you looking for me?" She glanced over her shoulder briefly to see Chase grabbing for his phone as it rang, still down on his haunches next to Zeke.

"Yes! I've got gobs of lavender growing in my yard, just gobs of it. Here." She shoved a freshly cut bunch into Grace's arms. "All the rainfall we've been getting has been enough to fill up our reservoirs and deep water the gardens."

The sweet and woody smell of the blooms in her arms conjured up memories that Grace had long thought buried. She inhaled another breath, allowing it to linger in her senses, barely cognizant of another distinct aroma. Something smoky, like a spice. Cinnamon, maybe?

Wren continued to gush. "I'm so thrilled to have someone to share them with again."

Grace smiled. "Thank you, Wren. But I bet many people living around here would love the bounty from your garden."

"Hardly! Most of them are weekenders, and none are like the Holloway family. No, no, it's very sad."

"What do you mean?"

She wiggled her hand through the air as if brushing away her new neighbors. "They are hardly ever here—those beautiful homes are usually quite dark. And when they do come they roll their beautiful cars straight into their garages. Not even a wave."

"I'm sorry."

Wren slipped her hand through the crook of Grace's arm. She leaned in close as if they were dishing on the latest news of the 'hood. "Tell me about your man," she said in a whisper. "He's a tall drink of something, isn't he?"

Thank goodness the flowers were occupying her hands. Otherwise, Grace feared the sudden onset of sweaty palms might give away her situation. "He's, well, he's a ... great guy." There. That was safe.

Wren gripped her arm tighter, steadying herself, and glanced back. "He's crazy about you, and that is so attractive in a man."

Grace kept her gaze focused on the roll of white, foamy waves a stone's skip away. She couldn't outright laugh at Wren's comment—how would that look? But she didn't dare agree with what she said either. Hadn't they already dug themselves into a deep enough sand hole that would be difficult to climb out of when the truth was revealed? No sense in agreeing with an observation so incredibly incorrect!

"Grace!"

Grace swung around and Wren let go of her arm. She shielded her eyes with her hand.

"Zeke wandered off!"

"Oh dear," Wren said.

"What? No!" Grace quickly scanned the water's edge and then back toward Chase. "Which way did he go?"

Chase shook his head and opened his arms wide with a giant shrug. "I'll go this way," he shouted. "You go down to the water!"

Grace handed the flowers back to Wren. "I'm so sorry. I've got to go. Will you keep an eye out?"

"Of course, of course."

Grace took off toward the tide line, watching for any sign of Zeke. "Zeke! Here, boy! Zeke!" How hard could he be to spot? He had fluffy black hair and moved fast. Surely one of them would see him soon.

After a half hour, Chase joined Grace in the area of her

search. More than once she heard him swear, while she held back tears that pressed up against her eyes and windpipe.

She couldn't lose Zeke. Finding him had meant more to her than she could ever have imagined. She hadn't planned on that, but when she brought the puppy into her home, he quickly burrowed into her heart as well.

Chase halted in place and expelled one exasperated breath. He continued to scan the beach with his eyes, only now he avoided Grace's.

Silence dropped between them. A wave crashed. A gull sent out an alert for food. Chase crossed his arms and dropped his gaze to the sand below.

She turned on him then. "How could you let this happen? What were you doing when he slipped off?"

He raised his eyes. In them, she saw clouds and worry. "Nothing. He was digging away and then all of a sudden I looked down and he was gone."

"You looked down? From what—the phone? That's it, isn't it?"

"It was one call."

"No, you were working on the beach!"

"Oh, now you are one to talk."

She took a step toward him and lifted her chin. "What does that mean?"

He stuck a tongue into his cheek, staring back at her. "It means I haven't seen you take a break from that laptop of yours since you got here."

"So what?"

He shrugged as if he didn't care.

Anger crowded out her fear. "Stop deflecting. You said you'd watch him so I could talk to Wren. You promised!"

Chase shoved his hands into his pockets. His jaw hardened as if he were about to lash out at her with as much force as she was giving him. He looked her square in the eyes.

She refused to look away, refused to give him any grace at all. "I'm so angry, Chase. He's just a puppy. What if he gets hurt? I can't believe—" Her words died on her tongue, giving way to her first tear.

In a breath, he pulled her into his arms, molding her to him. She sank into him, her body warm against his, an imaginary line crossed. That first tear led to more, dozens more, until the place on his chest where she laid her cheek had become soaked.

She peered up at him and Chase's hand found the back of her neck. "We've got to find him," she whispered.

He nodded quickly. "Let's not stop looking."

She allowed herself one long, hiccupy breath before beginning to pull away.

He stopped her with a touch of his fingers on her chin, his face mere inches from hers, his eyes searching. "I'm so sorry, Grace."

Grace shut her eyes. He infuriated her ... yet, when had she ever been so content in a man's arms, so assured that this was where she was supposed to be at this moment in time? If only the circumstances weren't so dire—and she wasn't so angry with him!

She wiped away her tears with the back of her hand and stepped back, taking another look toward the sea.

Chase cupped her upper arms, his gaze assuring. "We'll find him, Grace. If I have anything to say about it, we will find Zeke."

～

THEY TRUDGED TOWARD THE HOUSE, their arms empty, no words passing between them. They'd been canvassing the beach for an hour with no luck at all. They'd repeated the question over and over again, but no one had seen Zeke.

Fog had rolled in, as it often did along this stretch of the coast, causing shivers to overtake Grace. She hugged herself from both worry and chills, with Chase close behind her.

The sounds of crashing nearby waves engulfed them, reminding Grace of childhood days spent at the beach house. She didn't love this particular memory. Grey never set well with her mood, even back then. Her mother may have loved all that cottony air, but not Grace. The fog rolling in often muted surrounding sounds while amplifying the surf. The monstrous sound of a wave hitting hard-packed sand only heightened her fears.

If only she hadn't let Zeke off of his leash.

If only she hadn't allowed herself to be distracted by Wren.

If only ...

If only she hadn't married Chase on a cruise ship!

Chase's voice broke her meanderings. "Did you hear that?"

Grace threw a glance over her shoulder at Chase. He stepped closer, his hand brushing her lower back.

"That," he said, whipping his chin one way and then the other.

A familiar whine managed to squeak in between the sounds of crashing waves.

Grace let out a whoop and scrambled up the stairs where Zeke sat on the welcome mat, the one with the dolphin on it, whining about how long they had taken to get there. His tail wagged so hard it nearly knocked a hole in the back door.

"You brute! I can't believe you're here!" Zeke slobbered all over Grace's cheeks and chin as she bent down and scooped him up, giving him Eskimo kisses. "I'm never letting you out of my sight again!"

Chase's gentle touch on her shoulder turned her around, and he encapsulated both Zeke and her into a bear hug. Tears that had started falling earlier fell even harder now, the tension of the past hour rushing out of her in a torrential crush. She heaved from a deep place, leaning into the relief.

"I'm sorry," Chase whispered into her hair. He continued to hold them both tightly.

Though her tears subsided, Grace kept her face buried in Chase's chest until Zeke whined as if to say he'd had enough emotion for one night. She pulled back and looked up into Chase's face.

His dark eyes were hooded as they took in her eyes, her face, and eventually, her mouth. She couldn't miss the charm of their comfort at this moment when dread had been on her mind only minutes before. "I'm sorry for yelling at you," she whispered.

One of his hands slid to her waist. As he leaned in, his eyes locked on her lips. She resisted the urge to give in to this moment, though the unwavering resolve that had seen her through endless nights of studying for the bar was nowhere to be found. She knew how much she needed all her strength to fend off what seemed like the inevitable—the salty taste of his kiss. The temptation was almost too much to bear.

Until a whine from Zeke startled her, wiping away the magic in the air. A weird sort of giggle escaped her like she was all of sixteen.

Chase continued to hold her, though his grip had loosened. His skin looked flush, a glimmer of that almost-kiss in his eyes. "I am deeply sorry." He swallowed, eyeing her. "I promise it won't happen again."

Maybe she'd misjudged him, had misjudged their entire arrangement. Perhaps they'd been brought together for a reason that neither of them had considered. Could it be that everything they never knew they wanted might be within reach?

"Grace?"

"Hm?"

"When did your sister say she would be calling?"

The video call! Grace gasped. "I completely forgot about it." Her heartbeat began to accelerate, and not in a sexy way. Her mind had to, once again, switch gears. Had she and Chase discussed the implications of their fake union thoroughly? Did they know how they would act? How they'd answer her siblings' questions?

And did he truly understand how much she hated keeping the truth from them?

Chase's warm touch on her cheek stilled her, calm flooding her nerves. She flicked a glance upward, taking him in.

"It's going to be fine," he said. "You and your family still have much to discuss regarding the beach house. I'll be there as your ... as your arm candy."

She threw her head back, a ripple of laughter overtaking her. "Perfect. Just perfect." Zeke took that as an opportunity to lunge forward to give her one more sloppy lick on the neck. After wrestling herself away, Grace exhaled, centering herself. "I have to admit that I can't wait for this call to be over."

Chase opened the porch door and stood back for Grace

and her beloved dog to step inside. "C'mon, let's go meet the family."

THIS WAS A FIRST. Four out of five siblings had signed in for the video chat. Grace and her three sisters, plus their brother, who had yet to show, had not managed to see each other for the past five Christmases. The only time they'd been together recently was after their parents' death last year. And then only long enough to say their goodbyes and go back to their respective bubbles.

"Did Jake say for sure that he'd be on the call?" her sister Maggie asked.

Though their Wi-Fi reception was spotty, Grace recognized the telltale sign of stress on her eldest sister's face. And worry. Her sister hadn't done well in the relationship department. As a result, she was raising a daughter alone, a niece that Grace had not seen nearly enough. Fittingly, Maggie managed to maintain her status of "mother" to their ragtag sibling group.

From her chic apartment, Lacy sipped her wine and smirked. "Who cares? Our brother's a flake."

Bella looked up from a book, something pink and flowery on the cover. She frowned, her big eyes peering over the cover and into the screen. "I think Jake is quite dashing. I would not be surprised at all if he's been delayed by something heroic."

"What? Like helping an old woman cross the street? Please." Lacy set her goblet down after emptying it and she huffed a sigh, sat back, and refocused on the screen. "So, big sister, tell us about your recent name change."

"Hold on a sec." Maggie reached forward and adjusted her computer screen, giving them all a close-up glimpse of her ample cleavage. Tendrils of thick, highlighted hair unfurled along her shoulders. She truly did have the best hair, being a hairdresser and all. "I want to get a better picture of the happy couple."

Grace rolled her shoulders, attempting to look relaxed. She turned slightly toward Chase and gave him a hopeful smile, then addressed her siblings, which wasn't easy since they were scattered in boxes across her computer screen. "Everyone, I'd like you to meet Chase."

"Welcome to the family," Bella said, her voice childlike. Bella had a way of looking at just about all aspects of life through a fairy tale lens, and because of that, her siblings had often compared her to Giselle in the movie, *Enchanted*. Grace half-expected to learn that bluebirds appeared in the morning to help her little sister slip into a sundress.

"It's a pleasure to meet you all," Chase said.

Lacy assessed him. "Did Grace mention she had three sisters?"

Chase hesitated. "I ... well."

Lacy laughed. "I knew it. Of course, she didn't! She isn't labeled the smart one for nothin'."

Grace ran a tongue across her top row of teeth, fuming. "It's not like we've seen each other all that much lately ..."

Maggie's phone rang. She frowned, picked it up, and glanced at the screen before shoving it back into her purse. "Knock it off, Lacy."

"Oh, I forgot how you like to defend our goody-two-shoes sister."

Grace reached for the keyboard of her laptop. "Maybe this wasn't such a good idea."

Maggie shook her head. "Forget about Lacy's nonsense. How's the old place?" she asked, her expression suspicious. "Probably needs a ton of work, right?"

Chase relaxed on the couch and casually put his arm around Grace's shoulder. Grace suspected he was glad that attention had already turned to the beach house. She was too. "Not really. Seems like it's in pretty solid shape. We've been enjoying ourselves immensely."

Lacy's laugh broke through the pleasantries. "Oh, I just bet you are!"

Bella shushed her, while Maggie shot a *really?* at their middle sister, turning her head slightly as if they were actually in the same room.

Lacy brushed a strand of hair from her face and tucked it behind her ear. "I, for one, would like Jake to get his butt over there soon to assess the house's needs. The idea that lovebirds can give us any kind of honest assessment is just, well, it's pretty dumb, if you ask me."

Grace clenched a hand. "Are you calling me a liar?"

Chase cleared his throat. She glared at him before turning back to her sisters. "I mean, are you calling Chase a liar?"

Chase coughed out a laugh, as if to say, *leave me out of this.*

Lacy collapsed into the sofa. "Always so dramatic, Grace! No one's calling anyone a liar—sheesh. Don't be such a goody-goody." She sat up again and looked pointedly at the screen. "Let's cut to the meat, shall we? That house ... I think I speak for all of us when I say that, though we had some good times there, I think we should each put in our time, stick on as many bandages as we can, then cut our losses and call that real estate agent who practically owns the town."

Bella, who had been holding that book in front of her nose the entire time, slowly set it on her lap. Wide-eyed, she said, "You mean sell our family home?"

Maggie spoke to Bella. "The family home was gone a long time ago, honey."

Grace stiffened. She sensed Chase's attention on her, but she ignored it. Still, he reached over and laid his hand on one of hers, a sweet sign of solidarity.

Maggie's phone rang again. This time she yanked it from her purse and moved out of view, terse-sounding whispers echoing in the background.

Bella continued. "I would just like to say that this is one of the few times we have all had to discuss our family's remaining home. Well, Jake's not here, of course, but you know what I mean." She closed her eyes, a diminutive smile drifting onto her face. "Think about the days we spent there when we were young. Really think about them!"

Lacy rolled her eyes. "I'd rather think about the root canal I have scheduled for next week."

Grace shook her head. "Lacy ..."

Bella cut in, those big eyes of hers open wide again. "C'mon, you guys. Let's all stop for a few seconds and reflect on what it would mean to sell it. Please?"

Maggie entered the space again and sighed. "Bella, honey, I would love to entertain the idea of keeping the place, but it's all I can do to put macaroni and cheese on the table each night. I need the money. I'll never understand why our parents didn't just leave us the place without these ridiculous restrictions, but they did, so I'm counting the days until we've fulfilled them all and can sell."

Grace saw the weariness in Maggie's eyes, the determination in Lacy's expression, and heard the wistfulness in Bella's voice. Her agreement with Chase had certainly granted her some time—though if he hadn't had to fire her in the first place, she wouldn't be in this situation. She bristled at the thought of being beholden to someone. Their father paid for everything in cash. Grace had always thought it to be a quaint custom, but now she wished she had paid a little more attention to his quirky ways ...

As if sensing her reflection, Chase squeezed Grace's hand. She withdrew it, feeling a bout of sweat coming on. Annoying little habit! She glanced over at him as her sisters continued their debate without her. He returned her gaze with a sort of curiosity, his usually tamed locks having landed every which way after the sea air had coursed through them. Softened his edges some.

The high-pitched clanking of glass broke her concentration. Lacy was holding her empty wineglass and tapping it with a spoon.

Maggie grimaced. "What are you doing?"

Lacy's right eyebrow shot up. "Really? Has it been that long since you've attended a wedding?" She turned toward the screen, nearly mewing. "The tinkling of the glass means the lovebirds have to kiss."

Grace scoffed, tired of her middle sister's antics. Truthfully, she was tired, period. The past week—and past few hours—had caught up with her.

"They don't have to perform for us," Maggie said, her voice agitated.

Bella cut in. "Oh, I think it's a sweet custom. You two do seem so in love, Grace. I'm happy for you both."

Lacy laughed and smacked her wineglass again with a spoon. "Here, here. Kiss her already."

Grace opened her mouth to protest when a strong hand

found her shoulder and coaxed her around. Or did she go willingly? Warmth washed over her, the same kind of heat she'd felt when they'd just found Zeke on the porch after an hour of searching.

But she had even less time to think about it this time around, torn between her desire to lean into Chase's strength, to explore what a real kiss from him might be like, and the reality that they had an audience staring back at them via three screens.

They were face-to-face now, his gaze studying her lips, then snapping up to her eyes. She stared into them, searching for something real, but knowing that what they had was anything but. Simply, everything about them was a farce. They were both just holding their breaths until the tumult died down, playing the role of a couple in love, though the truth was far from that.

One corner of his mouth lifted into a partial grin, and a tremor of shame reached her face. Her hands, as usual, broke out in a sweat. But he was going in for the kill, so to speak, and she couldn't stop him. No matter what, they had her siblings to convince.

In one breathless move, his hand firmly behind her neck, Chase dipped Grace away from the camera, and paused, lingering. The beating of two hearts intermingled with their breathing as they posed there, out of sight. Slowly, he brought her upright. Grace broke free from Chase's embrace, embarrassed by the slight gasp she made when they parted.

"Well, shew, woman," Lacy said, fanning herself. "I was thinking about a little peck on the lips, but okay."

Grace wouldn't make eye contact with any of her sisters. If this was how these weekly calls would go, she'd have to find a way not to be home next week.

"Grace?" Maggie said. "Let's get back to details. All right? Maybe you could start a list going, okay, hon? Jot down the things you think we have to fix right away and maybe we can all cobble together the funds to get those things done over the next few months. In the meantime, you can do some cleaning while you're there, hmm?"

Bella piped up. "Oh, but don't use dangerous cleaners. I'll send some cleaning solution that I make with essential oils. They do wonders—you'll see."

Grace pulled her attention back to the video chat in time to see Lacy roll her eyes. "Well, since our baby brother didn't join us tonight," Lacy said, "my guess is he'll show up there some night with a to-do list. It's not like he lives all that far away. And the man's an architect, for crying out loud. It's about time he picked up some of the slack."

The others conceded with a nod or a hmm. They agreed to meet again, same time, same place, next week. Grace's agreement was less than enthusiastic.

After her sisters signed off, Grace sat like a stone, the ocean's roar filling what would otherwise have been silence.

Chase rustled next to her. "That went well."

She lifted her eyes, taking in his chiseled chin, the stubble that had formed on his cheeks, and the way his gaze pretended to be all about her. "What was that all about?"

He frowned, those eyes of his darkening. "Which part are you referring to?"

She crossed her arms and hugged her middle. "Don't kiss me like that—or whatever— in front of them again."

Chase sat forward, eyeing her, his voice turning husky. "Let me be clear: If I'd kissed you, there would be no question about what had happened."

Her mouth dropped open.

He half-laughed. "What I meant was, isn't that what you wanted? You wanted us to look the part of the happy couple?"

She didn't say anything.

He twisted his mouth. "That's what I thought." He stood and offered her his hand.

She glanced at it, then back up at him. A few seconds of standoff silence landed between them.

Abruptly, he pulled his hand away. "Have it your way."

The walls were closing in ... Grace could feel them. Her emotions had run the gamut today. She couldn't let them rule her. When had she ever? No, she worked hard to meet her goals, but when she failed? She worked even harder to overcome her failures. That may make her a "goody-two-shoes" in Lacy's eyes, but she wasn't about to let her sister's criticism get to her.

Because that would mean giving up. And one thing she never did was give up.

Chase was pacing now, one hand shoved into his pocket and the other swinging by his side. When it came right down to the marrow of things, she didn't know the man all that well. That thought struck her to her core. Maybe she was living with a psycho ... a Jekyll and Hyde. Was that why Kate fled?

She glanced at him again and their eyes met. He stared at her for a beat, his Adam's apple bobbing. *Dang, he's gorgeous.*

With no words between them, he strode across the room, offered his hand to her again—more boldly this time—and she took it. He pulled her up to him like they were doing the tango on *Dancing with the Stars*. His chest rose and fell against hers, and he smelled of sea spray and sandalwood. *I wonder if Bella could mix up a blend like this ...*

"I'd prefer we not fight," he said.

She moistened her lips and rubbed them together. "Okay."

He peered at her. "All I was trying to say is that I can see that your relationship with your family is complicated."

She nodded.

"I'm sorry ... it appears that I've made it even more complicated for you."

Shoot. He was being kind. Again. How was that for a surprise ending to the day? Grace exhaled and shut her eyes. As she did, she sensed him moving closer. She wasn't about to object ...

A swift knock on the door sent her eyelids furling upwards. Chase let her go and made for the door.

Wren breezed into the living room. "Saw your light on so I knew you two would still be up. Here." She extended a pie toward them both.

Grace centered herself as best she could. She reached for the pie, warmth from the ceramic plate seeping through. "It smells amazing. Thank you so much."

Wren chuckled. "Just like your mama. She loved pie, too, but of course, you already know that."

Grace set the dessert on the kitchen island, grateful to turn her back for a moment. She hadn't remembered that her mother loved pies. How could that be? What other things had she forgotten? Grace pasted on a smile and turned back around.

"Can I get you something to drink, Wren?" Chase asked. He glanced hopelessly at Grace. "Water? Wine?"

Wren smiled. "Sounds like a miracle's about to happen!" She laughed. "Or maybe it already has!" Wren's arrival had awoken the beast, aka Zeke. Or maybe it was the aroma of a fresh apple pie that brought him out of slumber. Wren bent down to give him some proper attention in the form of lavish pets.

Chase looked positively uncomfortable.

When Wren stood, she shook her head. "Nothing for me." She pointed toward the table. "Oh, and your flowers are back at my house. I forgot them on the table."

Grace put a hand to her forehead. "Yes, sorry. I meant to go grab them from you, but after chasing our naughty boy down, we came in just in time to have a group call with my sisters."

"No Jake on the call?"

"Afraid not."

Wren frowned.

Grace put on a positive smile. "I'm sure he'll turn up soon. Probably stuck on some big project."

"As usual with that one. Your father and he, well, let's just say those two were like oil and water."

Grace nodded. This was something she did recall.

Wren slapped her hips. "Well, enough of my intrusion. I must be going now."

Grace stepped forward and grabbed both of Wren's hands. "Thank you again for the pie. I'm sure we'll enjoy it all week long."

Wren rubbed a thumb against Grace's cheek and gave her a pat. "Ah, you do that, lovey. Could use some meat on you, I think." She glanced at Chase. "Of course, a baby'll handle that pretty well, too, I should say."

Chase gave them both a look that was the dictionary's definition of awkward. Still, he ushered Wren out the door and stood on the porch to watch her walk home.

Grace twisted her mouth. Guess a psycho wouldn't have done that.

When he re-entered the house, Chase ran a hand through his hair. He looked at her. "I'm beat. You?"

"Yeah. I am."

He nodded. "That pie'll keep, I'm sure."

Grace let out a small laugh. "I'm sure you're right. No doubt it's fresher than anything you could buy around here."

"Well, then," he said, "goodnight."

She allowed her eyes to catch with his. "Goodnight, Chase."

Then she watched him wander down the hall, with Zeke on his heels, and slip inside his bedroom.

8

———————

Grace's mother always remarked on what a rare thing it was to have a child who preferred getting up early to lounging around in bed until minutes before the school bus called. "You're the only one of mine, child. The only one!" she'd said, more than once. Perhaps it was because she, too, liked to watch the sunrise in the morning. In that way, Grace and her mother had been very much alike.

Grace squinted into the sky from her bed, the sunlight from the east casting a glow through her window. With ease, she pulled the blanket off the bed and padded to the door. She stopped, pivoting on her bare feet. Zeke had draped himself over the edge of his fluffy bed. The only part of him that moved were his eyes.

"Wanna join me?" she asked.

With a grunt, he got up, did a couple of yoga poses while Grace waited patiently, and then followed her outside. She sat on the old pink bench and watched as the sun's distant light changed the color of the water from deep ink to a more sea-green hue. Just like those years she spent here as a kid.

Oh, how she wanted to go back in time, to those days when a beach sunrise was all she needed to feel carefree, ready to take on whatever this world foisted on her.

Her phone buzzed. A text from Mick.

Hello Mrs. Ryan.

It was her turn to groan. He continued:

Mr. Peters has called twice today. Wants us to send his file.

Judith says to ask: Should we?

Grace's mood darkened. From what she understood, Peters had indicated he'd be staying with the firm. She'd only been a lawyer for a short time, but she knew—his so-called "file" would be massive. This was not good. At all.

She flicked a gaze toward the water again, noticing that a cloud had blown in, rendering the ocean's color a notch deeper. Grace picked up her phone and began running her thumbs over the keyboard, then stopped.

Too much going on inside her head to make sense of it. Last night with Chase and her family almost felt normal. Almost.

Zeke whined. She slid a glance at the pooch, who chose that moment to open his little mouth as wide as possible. "I'm not hungry yet. You?"

He leaned his head to one side, considering. She laughed. "C'mon. You can wait a little, can't you?" She stood, grabbed a leash, and attached it to Zeke's collar. "I'll make a deal with you. Give me one quick walk around the neighborhood to clear my head and I'll add a chicken broth topper to your breakfast this morning. Deal?"

They wandered out to the front of the beach house and down the street where a mix of houses, old and new, lived in harmony. Grace's mind ping-ponged between the almost-kiss from last night, the one she could nearly taste, and the news that Peters wanted his file. She couldn't decide which to obsess on more, though, truly, one had risen to the top of her mind.

She squashed the memory of her close call with Chase with a firm swat of a virtual fly swatter and kept walking, Zeke in the lead. No sense obsessing over something that, last time she checked, was still make-believe and probably would stay that way forever.

Her phone dinged. Another text from Mick.

> Between us, something's fishy with billing.

> Check your email later.

She sighed aloud and shoved her phone into her back pocket. Pretty soon she'd have to remind Mick that she no longer worked for the firm, and therefore, didn't need to be in the know about the firm's billing practices.

Up ahead, a weed-strewn front yard led to a white gabled structure sorely in need of some paint and maybe more. She slowed, allowing Zeke to sniff along the edge of a broken picket fence that framed the property and her mind to wander back to blissful ignorance. As she did, she noticed the faded sign out front announcing Colibri Beach Church.

Of course. The little church they attended when she was very young. Grace had forgotten all about it until now. It had closed at some point, and from the looks of things, had never reopened.

If she allowed it, her mind could trail back to the Sundays when they'd come here as a family, she and her sisters in summer dresses, wearing their cleanest flip-flops, and Jake standing stiffly next to their dad, his hair slick—except for a cowlick that refused to cooperate.

Their mother always liked them to sit through the sermon, rather than dash off to play dodgeball or whatever the kids did during Sunday services. It's where they heard about forgiveness, love … honesty. Her thoughts lingered on that last word.

Zeke growled at a grasshopper he'd spied among the brush.

"C'mon, boy. You must be pretty hungry to be considering that grasshopper." She smiled. "Let's go back and I'll fix your breakfast."

She took one more look at the old church before turning around and heading back to the beach house. As she and Zeke trailed along, her mind wandered to the prayers her parents often said over them. Hearing them speak to Jesus in a normal voice, mentioning her by name, always gave Grace comfort.

Somehow, she'd forgotten about that.

The screen door of the beach house opened and Chase appeared, barefoot, his hair tousled. A ripple of something went through her, but she stuffed it down. She wanted to ask him more about Mr. Peters and what was going on there, especially in light of what Mick had told her. And she was going to need her wits about her to keep it all straight.

"Want some oatmeal?" she asked as she dusted off her flip-flops and followed Zeke back into the house.

"You making it?"

"Just like my mama used to."

Chase padded behind her and slipped into a chair at the island. "I wouldn't miss it."

CHASE HAD AWAKENED this morning to the blessed sound of the sea, a perk he hadn't known he needed. And then, just as hot oatmeal warmed his belly the questions began. What exactly was Grace's intent with her volley of questions over this morning's oatmeal?

"Tell me about Peter Mayer," she'd said.

"He's my dad's—well, our—biggest client. Long-time friend. But you know that much already."

"And he's staying with the firm?"

"I'm confident he will."

"I see." She dug into her oatmeal like a famished woman. "But you're not sure, right?"

"Any client can leave at any given time, Grace."

She looked up sharply. "Are you losing others?"

"Not if I can help it. As you know, I've been calling clients all week and Judith's done a lot of heavy lifting regarding our remaining accounts." He spooned up more oatmeal, but he was beginning to lose his appetite, his reality sinking like a stone in his gut. He didn't mention that he'd taken a late-night call from his lawyer who hadn't offered much hope. He dropped his spoon back into the bowl, then looked up to find Grace staring at him.

"What?"

"And you trust Judith, correct?"

He narrowed his eyes. Slowly, he said, "Correct." The

lawyer in him wanted to delve into her question, to turn it over and figure out the meaning behind it. But the guy who wanted to distance himself from something that looked like a real relationship didn't. Instead, with breakfast over, a walk on the beach called out to him.

Zeke joined him on his walk, but Grace didn't. Perhaps because he didn't ask her to. He trudged through the sand, a sharp pain in his back. Probably the knife Grace had inserted and twisted with each question.

Truth was, he didn't like being peppered with questions—he preferred to be the interviewer. Judith had pointedly told him that more than once in his life, and though he never enjoyed hearing it, she had stuck around long enough to share her opinion. And she did so often.

He wasn't, however, ready for Grace's voice to be added to the choir telling him how much he had screwed up. Frankly, he had already sung that tune to himself plenty of times.

Then again, he needed Grace to be on his side—especially where Peter was concerned. The last time Chase had spoken to his father, well, it hadn't gone well. Chase's heart dropped into his stomach at the thought of losing the one person in his life he could call family. He'd made plenty of friends over the years, but how many of those were simply clinging to his father's coattails? Friends with benefits, so to speak?

Zeke yanked the leash, pulling Chase toward the tide. Part of him wanted to get back inside already, to do the work he still had left on his plate and prove that he had everything under control. Maybe by then, his father's mind will have returned.

Chase blew out a haggard breath, his mood juxtaposed against the calmness of the sea. The other part of him wanted to wander listlessly with this mangy mutt until the tide washed clear out from the shoreline. He had already made several phone calls on this walk, spurred on by Grace's questions and mostly to former clients who had been dodgy with him.

He stopped and whistled at the dog, holding steady on the reins of the leash. Zeke pretended he didn't hear his master calling, but who was he kidding? Another whistle and the dog relented.

Back inside, Chase freshened the pup's water and fed him some kibble. He hadn't seen Grace since he walked in, but maybe that was for the better. They could keep their distance and, at the same time, keep their lives as separate as possible.

After Zeke was fed, Chase slipped out of his shoes and padded back down the hall toward his bedroom. The sea air had made his skin feel slick with oily moisture and he longed to feel a fresh cotton tee against his body. Grace's voice, coming from down the hall, filtered into his room.

"I understand. But I'm only asking for another month or so. Surely that's not too much to ask."

Chase flung his shirt onto the bed and stepped close to the door to his room. He had closed it halfway but hovered near the opening.

"Yes, yes, I understand."

She sounded disappointed. He wasn't sure what bothered him more—the fact that she wasn't able to negotiate whatever it was she was trying to manage or the reality that he was beginning to recognize the nuances of her mood by simply hearing the tone of her voice.

Her door opened and he heard her feet padding down the hall. Quickly, Chase pulled a T-shirt over his head, rustling around his room in a way that would, hopefully, give her the idea that he could in no way have overheard her conversation with … whomever.

"Chase?"

He peeked out his door, a forced look of surprise on his face. "Hey."

"Didn't realize you were back."

"Just fed the dog and was planning to do some work." He paused, noting the downcast look in her gaze. "You okay?"

She brightened, though the smile didn't meet her eyes. "Yes. Fine."

They both fell silent, and after a few seconds passed, Grace broke eye contact and turned back toward the kitchen.

With a sigh of resignation, Chase retreated to the back of the house to look at some discovery on the computer. He worked through lunch, looking up only when the phone rang. The sun hung over the water now, telling him he'd worked far longer than he'd realized.

"Dad?"

"Chase, my son. How are you today?"

Chase hesitated. His father almost sounded like the man he once was. He flicked a glance out toward the sea again, trying to reconcile all that beauty with the reality he faced with this phone call.

"Are you there, Son?"

Chase cleared his throat. "I'm here, Dad. The question is, how are *you*?"

"Pretty darn fantastic today. Aren't I, Amelia?" Chase could hear Amelia's muffled response coming from a distance.

"Well, then," Chase said, almost at a loss, "to what do I owe this pleasure?"

"So formal, Chase. Amelia? My son sounds like a prince!"

Chase could hear Amelia's hearty laugh followed by, "Then that makes you a king!"

His father roared and Chase was stunned.

Apparently, Amelia took the phone from his father because she came on the line. "Tim wanted me to tell you something we've discovered, Chase. We think ... well, we believe that some of your father's memory loss may have been caused by overmedication."

Chase's mouth fell open.

She continued. "Shocking, isn't it?"

"Unfathomable. Have you spoken with his doctor about this, Amelia?"

"Not yet. But two days ago, something extraordinary happened."

His father's voice piped up from the background. "I flushed those pills down the commode!"

Chase sputtered. "He *what?*"

"Don't shoot the messenger, Chase," Amelia cut in. "Tim is correct. He was disoriented and managed to spill an entire bottle of pills into the toilet. I've been trying my best to get the prescription refilled ever since, but there's been a delay, so—"

"So I didn't take them and now my noggin' is clear!" His father had somehow commandeered the telephone again.

"Dad, I don't know what to say. This is huge news, but it's also horrific, if I can be honest with you. I ought to get the medical board to take a look at your doctor's license ..."

"Enough about that, Chase," his father said. "I'm calling to ask how you and your bride are faring. You still making her happy?"

"Of course, I'm making her happy, Dad."

"Good. You married above your station, you know—never forget that."

He didn't know whether to laugh outright or wince, so he did some of both. His father had been smitten with Grace when they'd met. But after his condition had deteriorated so quickly, Chase hadn't been sure about how much Dad remembered about Grace. If anything.

"Well, that's all I wanted to know. Amelia," he shouted, "I'll have my dinner now ..."

With that, the phone went dead. Chase sat a long while, thinking about his father's phone call. Could it be true? That what looked like dementia might actually be the result of over medication?

He shook his head slowly. It was unthinkable ... malpractice ... and quite possibly, a miracle.

ARE YOU HUNGRY? Grace stood in front of the island as Chase wandered out to the living room, still thinking about his father's phone call. He and Grace stood on precarious ground and he had yet to figure out how to continue their ruse in the smoothest way possible.

She continued. "Was thinking we could have leftover spaghetti."

At her suggestion for dinner, Chase's stomach growled. "Sounds great."

"I'll get it started."

She padded back into the kitchen, offering him a few more minutes of relief. Still much to turn over in his mind. In addition to his father's possibly good news—he didn't want to get his hopes up too high just yet—another thought needled him.

What was she hiding? He knew that her parents had left her nothing except this drafty house—and only a fifth of that, with conditions attached. Was she that in trouble financially that the money he had paid her wasn't enough?

Earlier she had dumped out her wallet, counted the coins, scooped them into her hand, and jingled them around for a bit, so loudly in fact that she'd nearly woken him fully. He vaguely recalled her saying something about going out, but he was drifting off to sleep on the couch at the time—something he'd prefer to deny but at this moment could not. She hadn't even mentioned to him that they were all out of dog food. Instead, she'd conjured up all the money she had and spent it on the animal.

Hmm. What about the money he had paid her? Was she going to start strong-arming him for more? Dread formed in his gut, memories of his mother—a title that bothered him to bestow upon her—grinding through him. His father had loved her once, but where did that get him?

Chase put on his slippers and wagged his head. He reminded himself once again that he had work to do to keep this ruse alive. It was the only way to meet his father's requirements and gain back what was rightfully his.

"Dinner's ready, Chase."

Grace's voice rang out in the coming darkness. He sat a few seconds longer and steadied his breathing, regret washing over him.

If only he could trust her.

IF ONLY SHE could trust him.

Grace shook away the thought and gave the leftover sauce another quick stir, wishing she hadn't checked her email this afternoon. Mick was raising more questions about Chase's billing practices, and though it shouldn't concern her—it did. Like it or not, some emails make it appear that she was fake-married to a guy who blithely overcharged his clients. And then he acted surprised when some jumped ship with Kate!

She sucked in a breath, calming herself down. Though technically this wasn't her problem since she wasn't employed by the firm anymore, she had to wonder—was Chase using the money he supposedly made from unsuspecting clients to pay her?

And what if he was caught? Would he—technically, her husband—be going to jail? And if it was discovered that she was benefitting financially from his illegal ways, might she be implicated too?

What if he asked for the money back? No way that could happen, since it was already spent.

She exhaled and wiped her sweaty hands on a nearby towel. After, Grace grabbed tongs and began dishing up noodles to each plate.

"You don't have to do that for me," he said from behind her.

Grace's hand froze in the air above the pot of noodles. Her face flushed hot. Why was she not only cooking for him but serving him his dinner, too?

She turned and tried to hand him the tongs.

He flashed his palms. "Go ahead and feed yourself first. I'll wait."

Silently, she added noodles and sauce to her own plate, then handed him the tongs.

His eyes caught with hers, and then he quickly took the tongs from her hands.

On her way to the table, she grabbed an apple from a bowl on the island. Minutes later, Chase sat across from her. She could barely look at him.

"How's that list coming along?"

She looked up, dragging her gaze to meet his.

He swallowed a swirl of spaghetti. "The list of fixes your sisters mentioned last night?"

"Oh. That."

He glanced about. "Probably would be a good idea to update some things to get a good price for the place."

"If we sell it."

He raised a brow. "Pretty much sounded like a done deal last night."

She stabbed at a pile of noodles. "Nothing's a done deal."

He stared at her wordlessly. Slowly, he lowered his fork and scooped up more dinner. "I suppose not. I'm sure your brother will want to weigh in."

Grace looked up from her plate. "How did your efforts for the firm go today?"

He knit his brows together. "Excuse me?"

"You made some calls while you were out with Zeke. Right?"

He pursed his lips and nodded, his eyes not meeting hers. "I made a few."

She tried not to roll her eyes. He'd been on the phone for days, it seemed. "So you're saying that there aren't too many clients left."

"I'm saying nothing of the kind."

"What are they saying to you ... when you call them?"

"Who's them?"

Grace sat back and folded her arms. Hunger fled. "The clients who left with Kate. You are challenging that, right? And if you're not, why aren't you?"

"What's this all about, Grace?"

"I don't know what you mean."

"I mean, all this questioning. First all the questions about Peter this morning, and now you're grilling me about my business."

"I wasn't grilling. Just making conversation."

He raised both his brows now and clicked his jaw, as if annoyed. "Maybe we're playing our roles a little too perfectly. Don't get me wrong—I'm enjoying the beach. Haven't relaxed this much in years." He kept his gaze elsewhere before pulling it back to her. "But if it weren't for your requirement to stay here for a month, we'd—"

"Be living separate lives?"

He shrugged. "Yeah."

The fact that he did not come close to answering any of her questions was not lost by his sudden pronouncement. Not in the least. He was dodging, and she wanted to know why.

She rose from the table, taking her half-eaten dinner with her, but leaving the apple behind. "I'd love to release you, Chase, but it'll be hard to explain to my sisters why my new husband didn't even finish out the honeymoon." She tossed her dish and fork into the sink with a clatter. Through the kitchen window, she could see her neighbor puttering on her front porch, a glow of something in her hand. Grace lowered her voice. "Wren might suspect something's up too."

Chase brought his empty dish to the counter. "I'll clean up the dishes later."

Grace took a step back, keenly aware of his body so close to hers.

Chase didn't move away. "Look, as I've said before, I can get plenty of work done from here, so I'll stay awhile longer." He glanced out the window just as Wren caught sight of them both and raised a hand in a wave.

He waved back, leaning closer to the window. "Is that a cigar she's smoking?"

Grace stepped toward the window, careful not to allow her body to touch his. She squinted. "It appears so. Now that I think about it, Wren did join my father and her husband for a smoke on occasion."

Chase raised a brow.

"What? A lady can't smoke a cigar? What is this, 1912?"

Zeke careened into the room, yelping.

Grace broke eye contact with Chase and squatted down. "What is it, little guy?" She petted his fur, though he hardly gave her an out. He pushed his head into her palm, begging for more attention.

"Guess he didn't get enough of a walk today," Chase said.

Grace sighed. "I doubt that. He just needs some love."

"If you say so."

Grace scooped up the pup and tucked him under her arm. Nothing like a besotted companion to cheer her up. She almost laughed at the thought, but kept it to herself. From beneath her eyelids, she glanced at Chase, who had settled into her father's old easy chair with his computer on his lap. He had his companion and she had hers.

With a sigh, Grace opened a small drawer at the far end of the kitchen. To her, that drawer had always seemed like an afterthought, as if the builder had a tiny bit more room and thought, *What the heck? Why not just make a skinny drawer?*

She needed old-fashioned pen and paper to start making her "honey-do" list—though Jake, if he ever did show his face around here, would no doubt find that moniker annoying.

She rooted around in the drawer with one hand, trying not to stab herself on errant paper clips, the occasional tack, and other oddities in the drawer. Her hand landed on a ballpoint pen. She pulled it out of the drawer, clicked the button at the end a few times, and gave it a try on a piece of scratch paper, which in this case was nothing more than the torn end of an expired coupon.

Success.

While Zeke snuffled into her armpit, she dug around for a notepad. Her hand landed on something thick. She pulled it out of the drawer.

Instead of being a notepad, though, it was a small manilla envelope with familiar-looking handwriting. She squinted at the faint writing, realizing the word written was … her name.

Grace flashed a look at Chase who was concentrating on the screen in front of him. She swallowed and flipped open the envelope. A key fell out and bounced across the counter.

Chase looked up and their eyes met. "Everything okay over there?" he asked.

She nodded. "Yes, of course. Found a pen. That's all."

He hummed a response and put his attention back on his work.

Grace set Zeke on the floor and returned the key to the envelope. She slipped the envelope into her back pocket and headed to her old bedroom with Zeke sniffing at her feet.

She could not think of why there'd be a key in a drawer —and particularly with her name on it, nor why it hadn't been noticed by anyone before. But Grace hoped that by the night's end, she would find the lock her key would open— and what was inside.

9

———

Grace had laid awake most of the night, wracking her brain about the key, but couldn't think of what it opened or why there weren't any in her siblings' names. Their parents' lawyer had made it clear there was virtually nothing left of their estate, well, other than the beat-up old beach house.

She'd texted Maggie, figuring she might have some idea, but all she got back was: *Who knows? Probably an old key from some long-ago trinket in the house we lost.*

The house they'd lost. She hated to think about that, even after all these years. The loss of their first home to fire had changed their parents, had changed them all somehow. It was as if her mother's slow mental demise began with the very first flicker of flame. She rarely allowed herself to think about that time in their history. And she never, ever spoke about it.

Morning light came and Grace sighed, resisting the day. Waves rolled onto shore, calling to her, so with Zeke dancing beside her, she put on a hat, pulling her hair into a ponytail that stuck out of the back. Then she slipped into workout clothes, and after brushing her teeth, headed out the door at the end of the hall.

Bright sunshine greeted her, as did a familiar voice.

"Good morning." Chase swiveled around from his spot on the first step, a hat pulled low on his head.

"Hey." Grace second-guessed her decision to step outside without even a touch of powder. Vain, much?

Zeke hopped about, yelping up at her. She bent down and quickly hooked his leash to his collar.

Chase continued to peer up at her. "May I join you?"

She shrugged. "Sure."

Together they took off down the steps and over mounds of thick sand. They slowed when they reached the wet expanse of the wide, flat beach.

"Did you make progress last night?" Chase asked.

She glanced at him, squinting, wishing she'd remembered to wear her sunglasses. He was awfully concerned about the dreaded list she had been charged with making.

Grace exhaled. "I made note of a few things. You know, the obvious, like carpet that needs to be pulled up and replaced, and faucets in both the bathroom and kitchen." She didn't mention that she'd yet to go upstairs to assess the bedroom and bath up there.

He nodded. "Good. I noticed the leak when I was cleaning up the dinner dishes."

"My siblings and I should probably discuss the budget before the list gets too out of hand. Of course, Jake should be able to save us all some money."

"How so?"

"He's an architect, so ..."

"I hate to tell you this, but being an architect doesn't necessarily make someone a construction expert."

Grace gasped. She turned a look on him, slowing her gait. "You'd better not say that to my brother when you meet him."

Chase let out a small laugh. "I'm sure he'd agree with me."

She shook her head. "No, he wouldn't." Grace sighed. "I guess I never mentioned this, but my father was a builder. He and Jake butted heads over my brother's career choice."

Chase frowned. "Your father didn't want Jake to become an architect?"

"Nope. Thought he was selling out somehow. My brother had all kinds of wild ideas. He was a regular George Bailey."

Chase turned a questioning glance at her.

"You know, from the movie *It's a Wonderful Life*?"

"Right."

"Anyway, Jake worked alongside our father quite a bit, enough to wield a hammer and nail with the best of them, I'd say. But, in the end, he had big ideas and dreams that my father thought of as wasteful."

"Wow."

"Yeah. Think of it this way. My father was a meat-and-potatoes guy, while Jake preferred grilled salmon and organic greens."

"Well, then, if that's the case, my guess is your brother has already made a list of his own for the house."

"You'd think so, wouldn't you?"

"Don't you?"

She shrugged. "I'm not sure what Jake thinks these days. He's been rather AWOL lately, even more so than the rest of us, if that's even possible."

"Have you heard from him since the video call?"

"Not a word."

They continued to walk along, the morning sun cresting from the east. If it weren't for the retractable leash, Zeke might have nabbed a few sandpipers for brunch.

After stopping for a few seconds to snort and sniffle at sand crabs burying themselves deep inside soupy sand, Zeke took off down the beach, nearly yanking Grace's arm out of its socket.

"Yikes!"

Despite the shock of pain, she laughed and hollered after him. "Stop it, you ... you animal, you!"

"You tell him," Chase said.

They reached a wide tributary of rocks and water made from storm runoff and Zeke splashed on through, yanking Grace along. Chase put his hand on her lower back and reached for the leash. He glanced at her. "May I?"

"Please." She let it go, relief flooding her.

Chase moved the leash to his other hand and gently took Grace's hand as they traversed the running water together.

His touch woke up something deep inside of her and she jerked a look up to find him watching her. A spark lit his eyes, but she looked away.

When they'd made their way back onto dry sand, she let go of his hand, hugging her arms to her midsection.

"Probably should have turned around back there rather than tromp through all of that."

He reined the pup in a bit. "Why? Did you think I'd let you fall?"

She sneaked a look at him from beneath the bill of her hat. He was serious. "Just thought it would be easier."

He pulled on the leash, stepping closer to Grace. He kept

his eyes on her as if he had something to say. He didn't get the chance.

"There you two lovers are!"

A flush of heat swam through Grace's cheeks and she licked her lips, pulling her gaze from Chase. Her neighbor appeared beside them. "Good morning, Wren."

"Beautiful morning, isn't it?" Wren said.

Chase nodded. "It's paradise. By the way, that pie was delicious."

Grace's smile froze. Had they even bothered to slice into it?

"I'm happy to hear it."

She slid a glance at Chase.

He winked at her. "Had two pieces for my breakfast this morning."

Oh, brother.

Wren laughed. "That's lovely to hear. Listen, Grace, I'm wondering if I may speak with you privately for a few moments?" She leveled a look at Chase.

To his credit, he slid a look to Grace, as if for permission to leave her alone with the old woman.

"I'll be fine," Grace said. She glanced back toward the house. "You go on ahead. We can walk closer to the tide to avoid that runoff."

By now Zeke had run back to them, his pink tongue hanging sideways out of his mouth. Chase scooped him up and gave his noggin a swift rubbing. "I'll take this one back and get him cleaned up and fed."

When he'd gone, Grace turned to Wren. "Is there something on your mind?"

Wren slipped her arm through the crook of Grace's arm. "Oh, I hope you don't mind my intrusion. Trust me when I say this, but it's good for a husband and wife to spend some time apart on occasion. Makes 'em miss you more."

Grace nodded, but goose bumps alighted on her skin. She rubbed them away with her free arm.

"I was just wondering, dear, when your brother Jake might be coming around? He always was so good at helping your father fix things up."

Grace measured her response. No sense telling anyone, even Wren, about her parents' odd requirement regarding the beach house. Then again, maybe she needed some assistance of her own. "Do you need help with something at your home?"

"Oh, no. Nothing like that."

"Hm. Well, I'm sure he'll be around. I spoke with my sisters the other night—"

"But Jake wasn't there?"

Grace stopped. She searched Wren's face. Had she told her about the call?

Wren patted her arm. "Well, I'm sure he will show up soon enough. You know, he came some after your parents passed, but then he closed the house up tight. Not a light on for months." She gave Grace a wan smile. "Until you and Chase decided to spend your honeymoon here, that is."

Grace nodded. Wren was lonely. Her husband had died, and from what she'd picked up over the years, her daughter, Daisy, rarely came around. She'd heard Daisy had left in a hurry a couple of years back. Probably thought this small beach town too podunk to make an entire life here.

Hadn't Grace thought the same thing?

"You know, you haven't been by for some of my lavender lemonade yet. I would love to bring some by for you sometime. May I?"

A simple enough request, but why did it make a new set of goose bumps rise on her arms? An odd foreboding wound its way inside Grace's mind, but she shook it away, annoyed by her careless thoughts.

"Of course, you can." She patted Wren's arm. "You were my mother's friend, and I'd love to talk to you about her sometime. Would that be okay?"

Wren half-smiled and began to blink, her eyes watering. "Of course. That—that would be lovely."

They walked in silence until the Holloway house was in view. Grace stopped to say her goodbyes. "I'm heading inside for coffee, but I'll see you sometime soon."

She pulled her arm away, but Wren grabbed onto it. The wind rustled the old woman's greying black hair, and her eyes shone dark beneath a sudden cloud. "You do know, dear, that your sweet mother was, well, she was quite ... eccentric at times."

Where had that come from all of a sudden?

"I'm aware that my mother wasn't quite herself the last few years of her life. That's what you mean, right?"

Wren gave her that half-smile again. She nodded her head in agreement and let go of Grace's arm. "Goodbye, Grace."

Grace trudged toward the back steps, turning once to wave at Wren, who stood rooted in the sand, a sad frown pulling at her lips as if she had just lost her best friend.

GRACE STEPPED INSIDE THE HOUSE. A shower called to her, but the cry of coffee came through much louder. She approached the kitchen and halted, surprised. An almost-full pot of dark coffee, hot and steaming, sat on the counter. It made overtures she couldn't resist and she lunged for an empty mug.

"Lunch sounds fantastic. You name the place."

Grace spun around. "I haven't even had break—"

Chase's back was to her. He sat on the couch, his cell phone embedded in his ear, lost in conversation.

She swallowed back her reply and moved toward that pot of coffee. *Embarrassing.*

He was chuckling now and she snapped another look in his direction. He did not appear to notice she had reappeared in the house. *Thankfully.* Grace poured some of the hot brew into a mug and skipped the cream. Despite a brisk walk under the warm sun, she felt tired. Groggy almost. Lack of deep sleep could do that to a person.

She glanced at her reflection in the toaster. Eyes underscored with dark circles stared back at her. Ugh.

"Sounds perfect." Chase paused, then gave a low laugh. "No, no. I'll pick you up. It will be my pleasure."

Grace leaned her back against the counter breathing in the intoxicating liquid caffeine and staring at the back of Chase's head. Who was he talking to?

"Great. See you then, beautiful." He hung up and let out a whoop.

Grace squinted at his mop of hair. Really? He was making a date while they were cooped up together? She watched as he got up from the couch, stopped mid-stride, and began putting notes into his phone.

She cleared her throat and he looked up so sharply and with such pain etched on his face that she suspected his neck might have spasmed.

"Oh, you're there," he said.

"I am."

He replaced surprise with benign regard. "How was your walk with Wren?"

She shrugged. "Fine. She wants to bring us some lemonade."

"Today?"

"Maybe." She set her mug on the counter and snagged him with a look. "Would that be a problem?"

He slipped his phone into his back pocket. "Could be. I, uh, just made plans to meet a client."

She smiled. "Really? You have a client in this area?"

He leveled a gaze at her. "As a matter of fact, yes. Well, she's not too far away from here. We're having lunch."

"I see."

He lowered his nose and looked up at her like she was a wayward child. "You have a problem with that?"

Grace quirked her lips and turned up her hands. "You could just be honest with me, you know."

"I am being honest with you."

"Uh-huh."

He expelled a breath and looked down at the ground before whipping his gaze back to hers. "What's this about, Grace?"

"Do you usually address your clients as beautiful? Wait. Let me rephrase that ... can you name any professional in this day and age who addresses a client by the word *beautiful* rather than her actual name?"

He snorted, then scratched his head, eyeing her like she was the one who'd lost her head.

Grace clucked her tongue and said, "That's what I thought."

Fire stoked in him now. She could see it in the hard

angles of his expression. He glared at her while striding into the kitchen, stopping feet short of where Grace stood. "You're jealous."

Grace spat out a laugh. "Hardly."

They were chin-to-chin now, his eyes round but smaller than usual. He kept them trained on her. "Then why do you care what I call her?"

She held his stare. Why should she be the one to back down? "I don't." She thrust a fist into her hip. "But I also don't like men who cheat on their wives."

He threw his head back in a fit of frustrated laughter. "Oh, come on! How can I be accused of cheating?" He was gritting his teeth now. "This isn't even a real marriage!"

She jabbed her left hand in front of his face, the one with the wedding ring on it. "That's not what the world thinks!"

Chase took her hand as if he were going to shove it away, but froze, his thumb on her skin. He eyed the ring on her finger. It was as if time stopped, silence and thought co-mingling between them. Gently, he lowered her hand, releasing her arm to hang by her side.

Even after he let her go, her skin tingled from his touch, a flush of warmth lingering. He was still close to her, close enough to see the exaggerated rise of his chest and its inevitable fall. She wicked a look upward, into his eyes, their color a mixture of emerald and sage.

"Grace."

Her name on his tongue spilled over her. She couldn't breathe. Or was she holding her breath?

His mouth hovered dangerously close to hers. His strong hands embraced her face, his fingers tangling with her hair. A quiet gasp escaped her as she anticipated his next move.

She both wanted to stop the clamor between them and jump full force into it.

And then, as if sanity and judgment quietly took over, he froze, She rested her palms on his sculpted chest, his heart beating furiously as she fought the dizziness. She'd never felt anything like this before.

What were they fighting about again?

He released her, his voice soft but filled with a type of emotion she'd not heard from him before. "Maybe this … this scheme wasn't such a good idea."

She stepped back, wholly breaking free from him. He watched her beneath heavy eyelids. And though she would prefer not to notice, his jaw had begun to do that clicking thing again.

She found the edge of the countertop behind her with her hands and clung to it. He was right. This whole thing was an all-around bad idea … a really bad one. Papers could be written on the stupidity of this idea, of the difficulty of sustaining such a ruse!

Still, how easy would it be for them to completely extricate themselves now?

"I apologize for how this is turning out," Chase said. "I should never have brought you into my troubles."

As the heat faded and reality washed over like cold sweat, she understood what he was trying to say. He had no feelings for her, other than as an employee. Maybe a polite friend—or one that offered occasional "benefits."

But that wasn't her. She knew that now.

Grace pushed aside the memories of the taste of his closeness, shucking off the heat that those thoughts brought to her insides. She had no right to think of him as anything more to her than ... a business partner. That had always been their agreement.

She turned away from him, her mug of coffee staring back at her forlornly. "No apology necessary," she said. "We're partners and this morning just got out of hand. That's all."

He groaned and turned her around by her waist.

She flashed her eyes at him and took a step back only to ram her rear end into the kitchen counter. "Don't you have a lunch to get ready for?"

He rolled his eyes. "Are you always this combative?"

"Me? I'll have you know that my mother called me a peacemaker in this family."

"Really."

She tilted her head to one side, reality coming back into view. "How about you? How would your mother react to you coming on to your clients?"

A beat of silence dropped between them until sweat beaded on his forehead. He dipped his head low, their mouths inches apart. "Don't ever mention my mother again."

She shrank back, taking in the wildness of his eyes, pupils dilated. Was it from the moment that still lingered between them—at least for her—or because of something else? "You never mention her."

"She doesn't deserve mentioning."

"Because she wouldn't approve?"

Those eyes of his narrowed now. "Because she left my dad and me years ago. I haven't seen her since I was three."

Grace let out a gasp. "No."

His gaze hardened further, that familiar click in his jaw doing overtime. "Don't feel sorry for me."

"She abandoned you?"

He pressed his lips together, not meeting her eyes this time.

She reached up and touched the thick pad of his shoulder. "That's truly awful. I'm sorry, Chase."

His cheek twitched. "Don't pity me."

"I would never do that."

"Do you realize how good you have it? You may have lost your mother, but your memories ... I don't have one recipe from my mother. I don't even know if she could cook." He smirked. "Guess you think that's a sexist thing to say, too."

Grace winced, regret whisking through her like a cold wind. No, she didn't think that. Not at all. "I—"

"My father means everything to me, Grace. Nothing else matters." His expression flashed from heavy emotion to stoniness in a moment. He stepped away from her and she knew.

He did not trust women.

His mother had made sure of that. By the looks of things —by the casual flirtation with clients—she doubted he would ever change. She'd had her mind in the clouds thinking otherwise. She needed to shift this conversation, to pull it away from her growing feelings for Chase and toward what she'd heard. Before it was too late.

Grace cupped the mug of coffee, which had grown cold. "I know about the emails," she blurted.

"The what?"

The deepness of his voice, overly calm, caused a ripple of fear to snake through her. She questioned her decision to spill her findings at this particular moment. She rubbed her lips together before saying, "The ones questioning your billing practices."

His jaw stopped. He stared her down. "What questions about my billing practices? Who sent them?"

She hadn't thought this out well. She did not want Chase to know Mick had been forwarding his findings to her.

"That doesn't matter," she said. She took a sip of the cold coffee and tried not to grimace. "I'm just saying I know now why you don't appear to trust women much, and I guess Kate didn't exactly help you in that department."

He met her statement with silence, the kind that echoed.

"I mean, since she called you out on over billing your clients ..."

"That's enough," he snapped. He grabbed his keys from the island. "I've got somewhere to be."

She watched him turn and stride toward the front door, then stop and pivot toward her. "You know, my father told me that you reminded him of my mother, but I didn't see it. Now I do."

Then he walked out the door, slamming the screen door behind him.

10

Chase drove his Range Rover onto the freeway onramp at too high of speed. His surroundings were invisible to him, his mind consumed with ... his stupidity.

He ran a hand through his hair and grunted, then merged into the fast lane.

Why had he thought anything would ever change?

His cell phone rang. Judith. He punched the answer icon on the home screen of his dashboard.

"Yeah."

"Well, good morning to you, too."

He grunted a response.

"Everything going swimmingly, I see."

"If you mean I'm stuck in hell, then you're getting warmer."

"Ha! That was a good one."

He scowled. Good thing he'd had someone to confess the truth to. Judith knew about his planned engagement-turned-marriage and didn't judge him for his decision. At least not outwardly.

"Did you want something?" he asked.

"Well, yes, now that you ask." She chuckled. "I was calling to make sure you connected with Marjorie Winslow. I made a big deal about how I was going to interrupt your honeymoon to connect you two."

"I'm on my way to meet her now."

"Good. Now, do you want to tell me why all the bitterness? I thought your plan was working for you."

"Hasn't been what I expected."

Judith scoffed. "What did you expect? For Grace to give you all the benefits of marriage without the commitment?"

"Ouch. You make me sound like a jerk."

She chuckled a second time. "You do have a reputation, you know."

"You know that's not what it seems."

"And yet you've done nothing to dispel it!"

Chase sighed, letting silence drop between them for a few seconds. Quietly, he said, "I wasn't talking about sex." He was thinking about more—much more than that. Grace had opened up all kinds of considerations of the happily-ever-after kind than he thought possible for him. Reason number one why he had to leave just now. Had to get out of there ...

He changed the subject. "On another matter, Grace mentioned something about me overcharging clients. What's she talking about?"

This time, Judith sighed into the phone.

"Judith?"

"I wasn't going to mention this just yet, but since you asked, I've ordered an audit of our billing files."

"You ... what?"

"Hush now. Don't worry. My auditor is quite discreet. If he finds anything, I'll be the only one who knows about it. And you'll be next, of course."

"He won't find anything wrong. You should have talked this over with me, Judith. You know that I always review invoices."

"Wouldn't you prefer that I present you with all the facts first?"

He paused. "Are you saying Kate is behind this? That she did something to turn my clients against me?"

"For a smart man, you can be quite dumb sometimes. Yes, that's exactly what I'm saying." She huffed a breath that sounded like a weary sigh. "Chase, you crossed one too many women, I think."

He gripped the steering wheel. He'd lost his mind—he must have to have allowed this insanity to stretch over so many days, weeks. It was time for him to take the reins of his business, his life—no matter what his father's will might say. "I'll be back in the office tomorrow."

"How do you plan to do that?"

"After lunch with Marjorie, I'll drive straight home. Grace can ... she can ship my things to me."

"I don't think—"

He hung up on Judith mid-sentence, not interested in her reasons why his coming home right now would be a bad idea. He'd had enough. No more thinking. It was time for *doing*, though the strategy had yet to be nailed down in his mind.

One thing he was sure of—true love and all that sort of garbage was nothing but a fairy tale. A multi-million-dollar industry for storytellers. It had nothing to do with real life. Nothing.

His cell phone rang and he scowled. Judith on the line again. She'd saved his hide more times than he could count, which meant she could do him in for good—if she ever really wanted to.

But would she do that to him?

Reluctantly, Chase punched the answer button on his dash.

"You are not going to ask that poor girl to send your things. Understood?"

By the tone of Judith's voice, he could tell he very well may have pushed her as close to the edge as he dared.

"Tell her in person, Chase."

He hesitated. Instinct made his spine like a rod. If this were anyone else in his office, he'd send them straight to the unemployment office.

But this was Judith. She was a tiger ... and he a ball of string.

"Don't be so quick to write people off, Chase. You've been doing that since you were young." Her voice softened. "Constantly steering clear of sticky situations means you'll never have a chance of landing well."

Her gentleness, usually reserved for her children and grandchildren, surprised him. He swallowed back any thought of a retort.

Judith sighed into the phone. She sounded weary again, and the thought that she might not be around forever startled him. "I've been praying for you, Son."

The armor over his heart, already weakened by his pretty, make-believe wife, disintegrated even more.

"So you will go back to the house first?"

He released a sigh, the tension in his shoulders easing some. "Yes, ma'am."

"Good. Now, before you hang up on me again, Kate called the office looking for you."

He shifted, not wishing to leave the comfort of this moment. "Is that right?"

"Said it's important that you call her back. I played dumb, of course." She paused. "Did you really block her number on your phone?"

"Maybe."

"Well. Can't say that I blame you."

He grinned at this.

"Anyway, you might want to give her a call, if nothing else, to lambaste her for her backhanded ways."

"You want me to tell her that?"

"Not really." A sudden hardness tinged her voice. "Just find out what she wants and get rid of her. Think you can handle that?"

"I can."

"All right then. Goodnight, Chase."

He sat in silence, considering the schooling he'd just received. His equilibrium tilted like he'd put on a pair of prescription glasses and couldn't see a thing. Had Grace messed with his mind so spectacularly that he was rethinking ... everything?

Chase could feel that familiar clicking of his cheek, the pain of it crushing his jaw. His father had let himself go all in when it came to love with Chase's mother, and what had that gotten him? A heart full of scars.

For the first time in weeks, Chase considered his relationship with Kate. She'd come on to him first, telling him she was meant to have him. At first, he thought her a tease ... but then he fell. Hard.

He had his own scars to prove it.

He groaned, called up Kate's contact number, and hit the green button.

"Well, well, well. I had a feeling your minion would pass along my message."

"Kate."

"How's the wife?"

"Great. What can I do for you?"

"Not interested in chitchat. I understand that. Well, then, I'll tell you what I want: I want Mayer."

He chuckled. "Good luck with that."

"Oh? Haven't you heard? He only wants bonafide family men and women to represent him. Guess that counts you out."

Chase wagged his chin, groaning. "Kate, I'm on my way to meet a client. I don't have time for your games. As you know, I am a married man now."

"A fake married man."

"That's your opinion. Grace is ..."

"Yes?" The tone in her voice teased like she was a feline ready to pounce on some unsuspecting rodent.

"She's a special woman," *and she's mine*, he almost added.

"Special or not, she's not your wife and I have the proof."

He slowed behind a truck that had decided it was cool to crawl in the fast lane. Chase bit back a growl and switched on his blinker to change lanes, all the while wondering what Kate was yapping about.

He changed lanes and punched the accelerator. "I don't know what proof you think you have, Kate, but an entire ship full of people could tell you that Grace and I were married. You missed a fantastic crab appetizer, by the way."

She shot off a tinkling laugh that would make bunnies scatter. "Oh, dear. *That.*"

"Yes, that." Why was she annoying him now?

"That, my friend, wasn't legal." She paused. "You did know that, didn't you?"

Chase swallowed. Marriage license—check. Judge officiant—check. Willing bride. A slight grin reached his mouth. Check.

He had no reason to question the legality of his marriage to Grace.

"Are you finished?" he asked. "Even if you aren't, as I told you, I have no time for this garbage."

"Hm. You don't know. What a shame." She pushed out an overly dramatic sigh. "You were in international waters at the time of your 'I dos'. So the whole thing is washed up—excuse the pun. Then again, of course, you of all people knew that."

"I've got to go."

"I see I've taken you by surprise. You can trust that what I'm telling you is true, Chase, but should you want verification of my findings, give Judge Cape a call. I'm sending him an email about this ... right now."

Chase licked his lips, seething. "I'm quite sure you are wrong, but if by chance there is something to what you said, I'll get it taken care of. So I suppose I should be saying thank you."

"You should also be saying bye-bye to Mayer. The minute he learns you faked your marriage to the perky new employee in the law office, he'll dump you as his representative. He is an upstanding business owner, you see."

"And the minute he learns you've been fabricating invoices with my firm's name on them, he'll block your calls too."

Her voice turned to ice. "You're grasping. Nothing you can prove."

"Watch me."

Chase expelled a groan and tightened his grip on the steering wheel. He'd have to call Judge Cape to see if there was anything to Kate's claims, but no matter the outcome, he had suddenly been reminded why he and long-term relationships didn't mix.

As he sped along the freeway toward a potential client—a client he would acquire by his own doing—he knew his dalliance with Grace, or whatever it was they had going, was over.

GRACE SAT on the floor of her bedroom, searching the space around her for any idea of what the key she'd found might open. She didn't hold out much hope for a conclusion, but it kept her mind off of her scuffle—and that embrace—with Chase.

She replayed the way he had spun away from her and slammed the door on his way out. Her hands began to sweat and Grace shook her head, quieting a chastisement that formed on her lips.

Still, she had known better than to believe that love could happen with a man who had a bad reputation the size of Texas. Kate had walked out and taken clients with her. Why would Grace think she was any different? That she could somehow tame the beast with a history like his?

She let out a garbled sigh and lay down on the floor. Zeke trotted over and began to slobber over her, his spit stinky and hot.

"Stop it, Z. Can't you see me wallowing here?"

Zeke licked her nose and she swatted him away, swallowing back laughter. At least she could still laugh.

Her pup crawled up onto her chest, turned in a circle—which wasn't all that comfortable for her—and settled onto her stomach.

She sighed, aimlessly petting the puppy that had found her when all was about to fall apart. The corners of her mouth tugged low.

Grace had let her guard drop and all Chase had done was kick it the rest of the way to the ground—and then run after the next cute thing to cross his path. She still couldn't believe he sat in her father's chair and made a date with another woman, albeit a client.

Even if their marriage was fake, that took a lot of ... guts.

And then ... he compared her to his mother!

A knock on the door interrupted her mangled thoughts and she sat up, sending Zeke clamoring to the floor. He whined beside her. The knock came again. Had Chase left without his key?

She jogged to the front door and flung it open.

Wren stood on the front porch, her arm outstretched with a pitcher. "Lavender lemonade! As promised."

The cherry-cheeked woman's smile countered Grace's sour mood. She forced a smile upon her face so Wren would not think to ask probing questions that could be impossible to answer.

Grace accepted the pitcher. "Thank you," she said. "Would you like to come in? Or we could sit on the porch under the umbrella if you'd like."

"Oh, my, it's getting a bit blustery. If your beloved doesn't mind, I would prefer to come inside."

Grace opened the door wide. "Not at all."

Wren followed her into the kitchen where Grace retrieved two glasses from a cupboard. She held one up in front of her guest. "Will you join me in a glass?"

Wren shook her head. "Oh, no. That's for you and Chase." She surveyed the living room. "Is he here?"

"No, not at the moment." Grace took a sip of the lemonade, hardly tasting it.

"Well, I'm sure he'll be back soon. I've seen how he dotes on you."

A sudden thought pushed its way into Grace's head. "Can I ask you something?"

"Of course, dear. Anything."

Grace put her glass in the sink and started down the hall. "Be back in a sec, okay?" she said over her shoulder.

She returned with the key and dropped it onto the island. Wren gave her a quizzical smile.

"I found that key yesterday quite by accident and can't figure out what it opens." With two fingers, Grace slid the key with her name on it toward Wren. "Any ideas?"

Wren pursed her lips. "Hm. Sounds like a mystery." She flashed a kind smile at Grace. "That's your mother's handwriting. I'd recognize it anywhere."

"Me too."

"You know, I loved your parents. I was so surprised when they decided to settle here after all those years of moving around."

"Did you spend a lot of time with them after they moved in?"

Wren blinked rapidly. "What have you heard?"

Grace tilted her head. "I'm not sure what you mean."

Wren patted her curls, her gaze not focused anywhere in

particular. "All I meant to say was that I saw them plenty—your mother as well as your father." She stepped away from the counter.

"Then you know Mom hadn't been feeling too well, right?"

Wren's face paled.

"Are you okay?"

She nodded, her hands clasped in front of her now, her thumbs twiddling. She cleared her throat. "I should mention that your mother spent a lot of her time going through the attic, purging things. She gave away a lot to charity."

"Hm. We went up there after they passed away, but there's not a lot left. I suppose I could climb up there again to see if the key fits anything."

"Yes, I think that would be a good place to start."

Wren grew quiet and Grace wondered if she tired easily, as her mother had in the past few years of her life. One of the pitfalls of having parents who started a family late in life—though she wouldn't change anything.

"I think I'll go now, dear. I hope you enjoy the lemonade."

"I'm sure we will." Grace pushed away from the counter. "Let me walk you to the door."

When Wren had gone, Grace sat at the old scarred table and took another sip of lemonade. She allowed the heavy-on-the-sugar drink to drizzle its way through her insides. Oddly, the aroma of lemon mixed with native lavender brought a swirl of memories.

Such as the pen marks in the wood made by her brother and father, both of who gripped their writing tools with the strength of Goliath. Even though the house had been rented out to strangers periodically, there were other signs of her family's presence around that table too. A swipe here and there from a pink highlighter—Bella carried those around—fine scratches from dishes delivered, and dark splotches from years of elbows resting during raucous games of Crazy Eights, a cigar hanging from her father's mouth.

Grace snapped a look up at the tattered map hanging over the table. A plain wooden cross was nailed to the right of it. Her father had said something to the effect that the Lord went with them wherever they went.

She'd forgotten that until now.

Grace stood and bent close to the map, noting towns and cities all over California and some in the Pacific Northwest that bore a red X. She bit her lip, thinking. Some marked places their family had lived, while others were new to her.

When she was little, after their inland home had burned down, they came here. She was too young to remember all the details, but it was what Maggie had always told her. Unfortunately, her father could never quite find enough work here, so they would travel to other places, growing shallow roots while he built a house or a room ... once even a gazebo. They never did buy another house to live in full-time.

She sank back into a chair, startled by all she had forgotten—the fun times spent with her siblings, the little church and the prayers said, her parents' love for each other despite the disappointments. It was all coming back to her, and though she was achingly aware of the quiet, a sense of peace draped over her. *Thank you, Lord, for the memories. And ... for not giving up on me.*

She took another sip of her tepid lemonade, another sudden memory careening into view.

11

———

Chase pulled into the driveway but hesitated to exit his vehicle. He sighed. She'd left the light on for him.

Probably just being polite.

Or maybe she was concerned about what Wren would think if she'd gone to bed and left the house dark before her new "husband" got home. He'd noticed the way the old woman seemed to be hovering, nearly always showing up when they were outside or popping in to say hello.

He rubbed a weary hand across his brow and stepped out of the car. A rumble of surf greeted him, as did the ethereal presence of briny air.

He was going to miss that.

Quietly he opened the door and slipped inside. He found her asleep on the floor; a halo of yellow light from a nearby lamp the only thing keeping him from tripping over her. She was surrounded by books.

He didn't know whether to wake her or leave well

enough alone. Too late. She rustled, addressing him in a groggy voice before he had a chance to decide.

"You're home."

Her words landed in his gut. "Sorry to wake you."

She yawned and pulled herself up to sit. She blinked at him.

If only she had stayed asleep, he could have packed up his things and fled. He'd have left a note behind, of course.

Instead, he stood awkwardly, watching the sleep fall away from her, those big eyes of hers growing larger still. He wanted to look away.

"So you've been reading," he said.

She glanced at the spray of old books spread out on the floor around her. "My mother saved these for me."

He squatted down and looked at the titles, most of them from the Nancy Drew series. "These were written before you were born."

She rubbed an eye. "I know. They were my mother's and she used to let me read them in the summers when we'd come here."

"I thought Bella was the bookish one."

Her mouth twisted. "I was sitting here earlier, and I suddenly remembered the books and how happy my mother always said she was that she had brought them here." She looked up at him, her eyes clearing. "If she'd have left them at our old house, they'd have been lost in the fire."

He paused. "Where did you find them?"

"Oh, that's what I meant to tell you. That key I'd found earlier? It opened one of the metal file cabinets in the attic. The books were in there."

"Wow. What a find."

"Yes." She wrinkled her brow and aimed a now-awake

look directly at him. "How was lunch? Or considering the time, I guess I should be asking how was dinner?"

He stood abruptly. "I got the case, if that's what you're wondering."

"No doubt."

He paused, rubbing the back of his neck with his palm. "Grace, it's late. If you really care to know my business, you might also be interested to learn that my new client, Marjorie, is seventy-six years old."

"The one you called beautiful?"

"Yup."

"I see. What sort of case?"

"We're filing a lawsuit against a vendor who overcharged her for multiple years." He didn't add this, but even her suspicious attitude toward him couldn't change the lift this new case had given him. He was back in the game.

She quirked an eyebrow at him and pursed her lips.

He pointed a finger at her. "Don't you dare give me that look. I never cheated my clients."

She shrugged. "Okay."

"Do you believe me?"

Undecipherable emotion flitted across her face, but she didn't answer.

He pressed his lips together for a moment. "Anyway," he said, "it's true. I'm not a cheat. I only came back to get my things. Grace, I'm leaving tonight."

She needled her bottom lip with her teeth.

He began to move away from her and stopped. "Before I go, though, I have something important to tell you. I'll give you some time to wake up more fully first."

"Tell me now."

He clenched his jaw, then relented. "Fine." Chase took a

seat in the old recliner and leaned forward, his elbows jabbing into his thighs. "It's good news, really. I think you'll be pleased."

She watched him. The expression on her face told him how much she doubted him.

"I spoke with Judge Cape today." He didn't need to add what precipitated his call to the judge, namely, Kate's venomous phone call. "Seems we're not actually married."

She squinted at him as if she thought him stupid.

He continued. "There was some kind of mixup regarding our actual location at the time of the ceremony, and because we were married in international waters, the marriage isn't legal."

She said nothing.

"Are you listening, Grace? You're free." He didn't add, *I'm free too.*

He expected to see elation on her face. She had mentioned more than once how much she hated lying to her siblings, and though she wouldn't be able to clear up that fib quite yet—they'd have to keep playing the part for a year—at least she would eventually be able to invite them all to her ... real wedding. To whomever that might be.

She began stacking the old mystery novels on the floor beside her. "That's amazing news," she said, not meeting his eyes. "Really."

He nodded. "Well, I came to tell you that, and to get my things."

Grace tilted her head up to look at him now.

"I've got to go back home, Grace. Have to face the mess Kate left for me."

She continued to stare at her stack of books as if trying to decipher what he really meant. Finally, she lifted her gaze. "You mean you're going to try to get your clients back?"

"Some, maybe. It's time."

She nodded. "Good. That's ... good."

Twenty minutes later, Chase stepped down the porch steps carrying the two bags he'd brought. He glanced back at the house. The sweet aroma of a cigar floated on a distinct breeze, and the light of the moon cast a blue glimmer across the beach. But otherwise, all was dark.

IT WASN'T LIKE they had ever been married in the real sense of the word anyway. Yet why, now that Chase had gone back home, did her sheets suddenly feel so cold?

A whistle of sea wind heightened the emotion that had kept Grace up much of the night. Unable to fall asleep, she pulled on a robe and headed for the kitchen. Wren's overly sweet lemonade inside the fridge made her wince, and she opted instead for a bottle of water.

Her laptop sat closed on the kitchen counter, so she opened it up and began scrolling through online job boards. Legal counsel for a wholesale corporation ... Associate attorney for a collection agency ... In-house counsel for an insurance company ... all wanting three-to-five years of experience. What had become her practice of searching for work had lost some of its luster for some reason. She shut her computer.

Across the room, her dad's old recliner sat forlornly in the dusty light. She padded over to it but stopped when she reached the pile of books her mother had left her. What a gift. Her mother's mind had been going, they'd all seen it, though none of them wanted to discuss it—or do anything about it.

Still, her mother had found a way to leave behind a message, one that told Grace: I remember you.

Grace picked up one of the books and took it to her father's recliner. She pulled her legs up and curled into the chair, opening the book to chapter one.

She read until her eyelids grew heavy and might have stayed curled up in that chair all night long if a harsh crack of wood had not awoken her as she dozed. She sat up.

Another slam jolted her.

Grace dashed across the room and peeked out to see the winds had grown fiercer, palm trees bending low enough to tie their shoes. Zeke appeared at her side and licked her ankle. He added a whine of concern to the sound of howling winds and became skittish, but as she continued to survey activity outside, she kept him back with her feet.

One of the old shutters slammed against the side of the house and her shoulders tensed. She'd have to add that to the to-do list she was creating.

Zeke whined again. When she didn't respond, he began scratching at the lower part of the door.

She was about to tell him to shush when she noticed the patio umbrella flailing in the wind. Shoot! If she didn't hurry, that old thing could fly off and pull the table with it.

She flung open the door and jogged toward the umbrella, her bare feet picking up sand and, possibly, splinters. Zeke nipped at her feet.

"Don't you dare run off again!" she scolded.

Grace closed and latched the umbrella, the wind like a whipping towel to her ears. One of the chairs on the patio had toppled over. She righted it, then stacked it on top of one of the others. She stacked two more, hoping that the weight of them together would keep them from certain destruction.

She leaned hard against the stacked chairs thinking about that. *Together they would keep from certain destruction …*

In her mind, she saw Chase's hand taking hers as together they hopped over that tributary that split the sand closer to the shore. Her father used to take her mother's hand like that when they would walk to the little church down the street. She'd forgotten all about that, but Chase's action had unearthed the memory.

It had seemed like a nothing moment at the time, a blink-and-you'd-miss-it sort of thing. But down deep, the gesture had melted the glacier inside of her.

Wren had interrupted them, and though she had willingly left Chase's side to talk with her old friend, a kind of "what-if" niggled at her. If they had continued walking together, their hands brushing one another, their eyes meeting … would they have connected on some deeper level?

Was that what she had hoped for all along?

A side table toppled and Grace leaped forward to grab it before it tumbled further and could do some damage. She stuck it upside down in a safe corner. As the wind permeated the fabric of her summer robe and continued to rattle the familiar old beach house, Grace realized she had things under control. Not one drop of sweat on her hands. The patio furniture had been saved, secured by quick thinking and maneuvering. If she had ever wondered whether she could handle life's storms alone, she now knew for certain that she could.

But is that all she wanted?

By Sunday, Grace had made a honey-do list that would make Jake's head explode. He had better show up to the video call this time!

Still, she wasn't sure what she'd be telling her family about Chase's absence.

From underneath the old kitchen table, Zeke pushed his nose into her calf. A few weeks ago, Grace's puppy had barely been able to nip at her heels. But look at him now. Hopefully, he wouldn't grow as large as Clifford the Big Red Dog. How would she afford to feed him?

He prodded her again with his nose, which tickled her with its cold wetness.

"Fine," she said with a grunt. She'd been working on a new project, following an inkling that had invaded her thoughts overnight. She bookmarked a website she'd been searching, then shut the cover of her laptop.

"C'mon, pup." She latched Zeke with the leash and led him outside, carrying flip-flops in her other hand.

She dug her toes into the sand, reveling in its coolness below the surface. Few clouds were in the sky, likely scared off by the recent winds.

Zeke trotted ahead of her, waves lapping their hellos onto the shore.

"Hey, aren't you Grace?"

The man jogged toward her, his arms thickly sculpted, his dark hair brushing his neck. He wore scruff on his face and a bright, white smile.

She had no clue who he was.

"Don't remember me, eh?"

She shook her head. "Sorry, no. Remind me of your name?"

He wiped a hand on his tank and stuck it out to her. "Luke. I knew your family when we were kids. Later, actually."

A light switched on inside her head. Of course. Luke Hunter—local surf champ and the love of Maggie's life. That's what her older sister had called him, at least for a time. After he broke Maggie's heart his moniker changed to No-good Hunter.

She huffed out a small laugh, remembering. That was all in the past. She shook his hand. "Of course. Sorry about that."

"No worries. It's been a long time." He paused, sincerity in his eyes. "I was sorry to hear about your parents."

She nodded. "Thank you."

Zeke trotted up from where he'd been splashing through waves and stood between them. After sniffing around Luke's feet, he shook, violently, spraying them both with seawater.

"Zeke!" Grace tried to hop out of the way.

Luke bent down and stroked the dog's coat. "Hey, buddy. Thanks a heap. Now I won't need a shower."

"Sorry. Again." She gave Zeke a scolding look. "At least it's fairly warm."

Luke gave her a good-natured smile. "For now. The wind's supposed to come up soon. Thought I'd get a run in before that happens." An awkward silence began to form. He cleared his throat and flashed her another smile.

Grace wrapped Zeke's leash around her wrist and took a step past him, turning around just long enough to say, "I won't keep you. Enjoy the rest of your run, Luke."

"Grace?"

She turned back around.

His eyes squinted in the rising sun. "How's Maggie?"

She thought for a second. Should she tell him that her older sister probably never quite got over him? That though they were only teenagers, it was true love to her? That she married the wrong guy and had a baby and now she's alone with a child? That she works sixty hours a week just to make enough money to live and provide?

Instead, she offered him a wistful smile. "My sister's doing great. She's the mother of a beautiful daughter—my niece."

He nodded, his face thoughtful. "That's great. Say hello for me to her, will you?"

Grace agreed that she would and restarted her walk down the beach. In front of them, sharp-beaked sandpipers skittered away at the sight of Zeke's laser-like focus. She followed along, aware of the shuddering sounds of the ocean on one side and the call of gulls overhead.

But she couldn't stop thinking about her chance meeting with Luke. So many questions. Did he still live here or was he visiting? What did he do these days? Married? Kids?

A breeze had kicked up. Nothing like the wind that had nearly toppled her patio furniture earlier in the week, thankfully. She quickened her pace. One thing she knew she wouldn't do was mention to Maggie that she had run into Luke. True, her sister had only been a teenager when she experienced her first heartbreak, but as Grace recalled, she'd taken it hard and did not need to be reminded.

Nor did Grace care to give Maggie any reason not to fulfill her obligation regarding their parents' wishes. If she knew Luke was around, she might try to stay as far away as possible. She'd have to warn Jake since he would be taking over the house soon.

Her phone buzzed in her pocket, startling her.

"Hello?"

"It's Chase."

She licked her lips and watched a wave sputter onto the sand and then rush back into the sea. "How are you?"

"Good. You?"

"Great."

The phone was quiet for a beat. "That's good to hear."

A wave rolled in, swallowing her feet. She bit back a yelp. "Was there something you needed?"

"Yes. I left a satchel behind. It's the smaller one—"

"Black leather, right."

"You've seen it."

"No, but I know the one. Anyway, I'll check your room and put it aside for you."

"Hm. I need you to send it."

"Oh. Okay." It wasn't like she expected him to return to the beach house, but for some reason, she hadn't *not* expected him to either. "I'll do that tomorrow."

"Great."

She held the phone to her ear, one part of her life leaning into the calling of the sea while the other half stayed caught up in the mess of the past few weeks.

Chase said, "How were the books?"

"The books?"

"When I left the other day you were surrounded by Nancy Drew novels."

"Oh. Yes. I've read four of them."

"Already? Four of them?" She heard a bit of a smile in his voice. "I'm enjoying the picture of that."

She was at a loss. Their past few conversations had been like riding a seesaw: high one minute, then down in the pit. What were they supposed to talk about, exactly? What was acceptable and what was out of the question?

Chase interrupted her musings. "Are you going to be able to handle the call with your family tonight? Without me?"

"Yes." She didn't have a choice. Did she?

"Grace?" She recognized concern in his voice. "What's that sound?"

She leaned her ear hard to the side, bracing her phone against her shoulder. With her free hand, she zipped up her jacket. "It's the wind," she said, reacting to the morning's sudden change of temperature. Luke was right. *Wind's supposed to come up soon ...*

"Sounds treacherous."

She chuckled. "I wouldn't say that. Not yet, anyway. Although one night last week we nearly lost our patio umbrella to the prevailing winds. I had to run around the place battening down the hatches."

He whistled. "I'm glad to hear you had it all under control."

Her smile dimmed. Is that what he thought? That everything had magically fallen together after he left? That his presence—or lack thereof—hadn't been felt?

Of course, he did. Because their relationship had been fake from the start.

Wind forced its way through the fabric of Grace's coat and she shivered. With precision, Zeke changed directions, leaped over a pile of seaweed, and began to lead Grace back to the house. Even her puppy dog must have decided it was time to turn around.

A second voice could be heard on the other end of the line. Followed by a shuffling of voices back and forth. Judith?

The timbre of Chase's voice changed from velvety to metallic. "Grace? I have to go. You'll send the satchel?"

"Will do."

Off the call now, she trudged up the sand toward the old beach house, thankful for the welcoming embrace of its saggy porch and warm insides. Because the instant his voice was no longer connected to hers, she knew.

Despite Chase's reputation, despite every warning sign that shot up whenever she thought of him—which was far more often than it should have been—Grace had fallen for her boss. She hated admitting it, even in the privacy of her mind, but she wanted him by her side. Now.

Only it was too late.

CHASE LEANED BACK, the satiny brush of Grace's voice still in his ears. He tapped his pen hard on the desk once, twice, a third time, as if the action might drive all thoughts of her from his head.

Judith jutted her chin through the doorway. "You ready?"

He turned toward her. He'd asked her to come in on a Sunday and she'd agreed. After church, of course.

Why did that twist something in his gut?

Judith stepped into the room, calendar in hand and a frown on her face. "What is it? More bad news?"

He shook his head and swiveled his chair around until he was staring at the wall. Then he shut his eyes tight, forcing himself to pull it together. He had work to do!

He swiveled back around and gestured for Judith to take a seat in front of the desk.

She adjusted her glasses. "You're scaring me."

He frowned. "How so?"

"I've never seen you so lost over a woman." She quirked her head to one side. "She's undone you, Chase."

He tossed the pen onto his desk and planted his forearms on his desk. "Got your calendar and the audit?"

"You know I do."

He stared at her and she at him.

Judith said, "First, as suspected, no one was double charged. That was just something Kate was saying to current clients, mostly the ones she'd brought in anyway."

"Except for Burns, Toft, and …"

Judith reviewed her notes. She looked up. "And Callaghan."

Chase sat back, the squeak of his desk chair like a cranky toddler. He steepled his hands, concentrating.

Judith interrupted him. "Burns and Toft have both agreed to meet you this week. I've added them to your calendar. Callaghan hasn't answered my calls."

"Forget about him."

Judith's eyebrow shot up. He knew that look. She believed that he was wiping his hands of Callaghan's case, walking away rather than dealing with it head-on. He almost laughed.

"I'm having lunch with him on Thursday," he said, finally.

"You're kidding."

"I don't kid."

"No, you certainly do not."

He shot her a look. "Anything else?"

"Not at the moment." She stood and stepped toward the door, stopping briefly. "I suppose you will be working late."

"That's the plan."

Judith nodded, though her expression betrayed her concern—she always hated coming in on Monday to the list of things he'd left for her over the weekend. She left him in silence.

Truth was, he'd been working nonstop since he'd arrived back in the city. How he ever thought he could leave this office to stay at a beach house with his fake wife was beyond absurd.

She's undone you.

Judith's words buzzed around him like a gnat. He flicked them away and then hunkered down and managed to think of nothing other than righting Kate's wrongs. Of working up cases that demanded his attention and of getting back on track with the doings—and undoings—in his office. He made five phone calls—left messages, mostly, approved Mick's billing hours, and studied his calendar to make sure he knew all that would be coming up in the next few weeks.

Three hours later, Chase stretched his lean arms behind his head, then folded his hands and cradled his neck. Leaning back, he stared at the ceiling. Grace's face, a tendril of wavy hair to frame it, stared back at him. He shut his eyes tightly, erasing the image.

A tinge of remorse sullied his mind. He'd abandoned her to face her siblings alone tonight. She indicated that she could handle it, of course, so why did it bother him so much?

A grumbling in his stomach reminded him he hadn't eaten much all day. Abruptly, he shook off his momentary guilt and grabbed his keys. He'd get something to feed his hunger and then come back for another blitz of work.

His gaze froze on the set in his hand, reminding him of the key Grace had found ... the one that led him to that treasure trove of books.

Chase shook his head slowly, remembering. Grace had read four of her mother's old books. He hadn't seen that coming. Not with her obsession with working and career building, and certainly not old children's mysteries. Tom Clancy novels, maybe.

The more he thought about it, the more incredulous he became. What was that like? To have a mother who thought enough of you to share her books with you—even after she'd passed away? He couldn't fathom it.

Thoughts of her continued to linger as he drove along the boulevard, its trees swaying, in search of a fast, grease-free dinner. He punched the "on" button of his radio, ready for a distraction from work—and from Grace.

Broadcaster: *"We're experiencing moderate winds this afternoon at 17-20 miles per hour ..."*

He pictured her on the front deck, her summer robe loose about her, her feet bare. She said she'd nearly lost patio furniture that night when the winds were far more than moderate along the coast.

He should have been there to help her.

Broadcaster: *"There's a small craft advisory in place tonight for coastal areas where wind speeds are expected to exceed 20 knots ..."*

Maybe he should call to check on ... the house. He punched in her number, then hung up. They'd already conquered several awkward silences on the phone today. No sense in climbing that mountain again.

Jake.

What if her brother decided to show up for tonight's call?

Why hadn't that guy shown up yet? She said she could handle her siblings tonight, but could she? Or a better question, was that how he should have left things?

Chase rubbed his neck. He checked the clock. Sunday traffic was typically light. If he left now, he could get to the beach house in a couple of hours. He might not make it for the start of the call, but he'd get there soon after. Then what?

He'd make something up.

"And farther north, Sundowner winds promise to make tonight a white-knuckle ride ..."

Chase's jaw clicked fiercely, pain searing his cheek. He glanced over at the burger joint off the boulevard, noticing its drive-through line snaking into traffic, and suddenly lost his appetite.

Chase switched on his blinker, changed lanes, and steered his Range Rover onto the freeway onramp headed north.

12

———————

"Honeymoon over?" Lacy mewed. Her sister reclined on her couch nursing a glass of Pinot Noir, a point she'd made from the start of their call. "It's the healthiest wine," she had said.

Maggie nearly clucked in response. "Zero wine is the healthiest, but whatever."

"Not at all," Grace said, breaking in. "He's a busy guy. Had some things to take care of at work, and well, you can't expect a sought-after lawyer to take a whole month off for his honeymoon, now can you?"

Bella smiled. "You are so lucky, Grace."

So far only her sisters had shown their faces on the screen, and though she had a mile-long list waiting for her brother, she rather appreciated not having to be on the receiving end of his third degree.

Grace continued, "Did you all get the list I emailed you? The biggest items will require us all to expend some elbow grease, but we should also repair some things—and outright replace others."

"Like those horrid appliances," Lacy said.

"Right," said Grace. "They work okay, so maybe we could sell them. To get top-dollar for the house, though, we should replace them."

Bella sighed.

"What's wrong with that?" Maggie said, clearly aggravated.

"They're such lovely vintage pieces that I hate to see them go."

Lacy spat out a laugh. "Vintage is a euphemism for old, ugly, decrepit ..."

"Stop it," Grace said. "Now, do any of you have questions while we're all here? Well, while most of us are here?"

"Yeah, has that nosy Wren been around lately?" Lacy said.

"She's a nice old woman," Maggie countered. "What's wrong with you these days, Lace? So grouchy."

"Why don't you ask Jake? He seemed to have some problem with her at the funeral. Couldn't get it out of him what the problem was, but man was he piqued."

"To answer your question, yes, she's come around here and there. Wren's been very kind, bringing me flowers and lemonade, that sort of thing." She paused, noting the distinct aroma of cigar smoke breezing in through an open window. Grace laughed.

"What's funny?" Maggie asked.

"Oh, it's just ... well, she likes to smoke cigars on her porch sometimes."

"Well, *that's* a picture." Lacy swirled the wine in her glass. "Are they Cubans?"

"How in the world would I know that?" Grace said, with another laugh.

An enormous rumble filled the air.

Maggie shrank back, her eyes wide. "What was *that*?"

Grace peered out the window. She had already made sure that the porch umbrella was closed and all the rest of the furniture secured. All looked good.

But wait. She opened the window more, listening, her eyes scanning past their property. She spotted a table toppled over on Wren's porch, its four legs sticking out above the railing.

Grace stepped back in front of her computer screen. "The wind's kicked up and I think some of Wren's furniture needs to be secured. I better go over."

Lacy scoffed, but Maggie nodded. "You go on ahead. We'll hold the fort here and discuss your list until you get back."

Grace grabbed her coat and dashed outside, just as one of Wren's plastic Adirondack chairs cartwheeled down her stairs toward the beach. The wind sprayed her face with sand, but she tackled the chair and carried it back up the steps, stacking it on top of another. She did the same with two more chairs, then she closed up the umbrella—shocked that it hadn't toppled previously— and picked up several small plants in lightweight buckets.

The distinct smell of cigar smoke lit her sinuses. She sneezed. Her neighbor's house was dark, but she called out for her anyway. "Wren?" Nothing.

She pressed her lips together. There was certainly nothing wrong with Wren wanting to pass the time with the taste of a stogie, but the winds were howling something fierce now. The scent of that cigar was strong enough to suggest that Wren, for some crazy reason, was outside.

A flash of a memory came to life in her mind. Wren's

house had a deck outside on the second floor—she remembered sneaking up there with Daisy, Wren's daughter, and dropping handfuls of sand on boys who hid beneath it. Quickly, Grace dashed down the porch's steps and jogged toward the back of the house.

She looked up. Wren was stretched out on a lounger, one foot dangling over the side. It was getting too dark to see much else, although it appeared that Grace had been right about the stogie. She could smell it. A faint red spot glowed between the slats of the deck.

"Wren?" she called. "Are you okay up there?"

Worried, Grace waited only a few seconds and then called out again. When no answer came, she headed for the back door, hoping she'd find it unlocked.

CHASE HAD MADE GOOD TIME. Even with the long phone call he'd taken from Amelia followed by his father. They'd had some news for him. He pulled up to the beach house and glanced at the clock on his dashboard. The Holloway family call started about fifteen minutes ago. Surely he wasn't too late to say hello and offer some semblance of support to Grace.

A gust of wind pulled his car door from his grasp, opening it wide. He exhaled harshly, shoving it closed after exiting the vehicle. Wind was whipping the garden flag Grace had planted. He jogged over to it and pulled it from its iron rod, tucking it into his coat.

Chase entered through the back door, the faint sound of conversation flowing from the living room. A sharp bark split the air and Zeke came running.

"Hey, buddy." Chase squatted to give the dog a pet, but Zeke leaped into his arms, knocking him backward onto his butt. He laughed. "That's some welcome!"

With Zeke tucked safely into his arms, he made his way down the hall to the living room. He didn't want to scare Grace by creeping up from behind but figured Zeke's intermittent barks must have alerted her that he was back.

The voices grew louder, but when Chase turned the corner, the room was empty. He peered into the kitchen. No one there. The sound of paper shuffling, humming, and a couple of words here and there filled the otherwise quiet space.

He stepped in front of the computer screen, Zeke nuzzling the crook of his arm, and found three pairs of eyes looking back at him.

"There's lover boy!" Lacy threw her head back, laughter bellowing out of her.

"Hi, Chase," Bella said.

"Hello, ladies." He glanced around the darkening room and back at them. "Anyone seen my wife?"

As he spoke, the words seeped down into his gut like a three-layer cake, surprising him with how good it tasted.

Maggie piped up. "She went over to check on Wren. Said the wind had toppled some of her patio furniture."

Chase stepped over to the window and peered out. It was dark now, but a soft glow emanated from somewhere behind Wren's house.

"I should go over and help," he said.

"Not so fast, lover boy," Lacy said. She pointed a half-full wine goblet at him. By the color, he guessed a Pinot Noir. "Did you really leave our girl alone on your honeymoon?"

"Lacy!" Bella said.

Maggie sighed. "Ignore her, Chase. You have to put food on the table. I think we all understand that."

"Shew," Lacy said. "Grace can do that all by herself, I'm quite sure."

The computer screen blinked, then went black, before lighting up again. A fourth box opened up. A guy with an expression that told Chase he'd rather be anywhere but at this meeting.

"What'd I miss?" he said.

"Jakey!" Bella said, her voice higher than usual. "We've missed you."

"Hey, Bella." He was looking down, away from the camera, as if multitasking. "Hey, everyone else."

"Hello, Jake," Chase said.

Jake's eyes snapped up and he looked straight into his webcam. He neither smiled nor frowned.

"You're the husband."

"I am."

Maggie cut in, "Now that the intros are done, Jake, where the heck have you been?"

Jake scowled.

One by one his sisters lodged questions at him, but Chase barely heard them. Instead, the aroma of burnt spices, perhaps cinnamon and cedar, reached him, his stomach roiling slightly. He looked out the window again, that glow growing bigger. He pressed his nose against the glass.

Smoke?

Chase showed his face to the webcam again. "Looks like smoke next door. I'm going over there."

"Should one of us call 911?" Maggie called out.

He opened the door, the stench of burning tobacco filling his nostrils, fear consuming him. "Yes. Do it!"

He tore out of the house then, running across the patio decking, then leaping over the short staircase to the sand. "Grace?"

A fizzle-like sound followed by silence greeted him. The dim light on his path went dark and he threw a glance back to the beach house. Black. He craned his neck to look down the beach where other houses stood. Not a light on anywhere.

Power was out.

A woman's voice cried out. "Wren!"

Chase ran up onto Wren's deck. "Grace! It's me!" He twisted the front door handle, and finding it locked, banged his fist on the door. "Where are you?"

No response. His heart rate sped, the throb of it pulsating in his ears. Another cry from a woman's voice reached him, though it was faint. The smell of smoke had grown stronger, tingling the insides of his nose.

He jumped down the stairs, ran around the house, and skidded to a stop in the sand. Fire was burning through a large patch of seagrass mere feet from Wren's house. The fire could sputter out if it reached the sand, but if it blew closer to the house? He shuddered, the force of fear hitting his jaw, which clenched so hard it ached.

"Chase? Up here!"

He spun a look upward. Grace waved both arms at him from a second-floor deck. "I can't get Wren to wake up!"

The deck itself must have been built ages ago, braced by the house on one side and two narrow wooden pillars on the other. The growing fire provided the only light, save a few stars. He had to get to them—to Grace—before it grew out of control and reached that deck.

"I'm on my way," he shouted, skirting the growing fire

and taking the back stairs two at a time. Surely one of Grace's sisters would get through to the fire department.

He reached for the doorknob and twisted it open with one turn. Inside the house hung heavy with the smell of old tobacco and the infilling of smoke. He coughed and shielded his mouth and nose with his sleeve. He hurried upstairs, passing a couple of bedrooms before he found the one with the deck off the back of the house.

"I can't believe ... I can't believe you're here." Grace flew into his arms, her breath hot against his chest. She drew back, her wide eyes filling as she blinked away the tears.

"What's wrong with Wren?"

She tilted her chin up. "I can tell that she's breathing but she still won't wake up. I'm so worried it's a stroke."

"Did you call for an ambulance?"

She shook her head. "I've tried using my phone, but it's dead."

He exhaled roughly, his brain trying to wrap itself around the past few hours. To think ... his biggest concern about coming back here tonight was a brawl with Grace's brother.

That... and whether Grace would allow him back inside her house.

A scorching wind gusted suddenly, wreaking havoc with their efforts to hear each other. Embers blew onto a rugged metal table and fizzled out. He snagged her with a look. "The wind's shifting. You have to go!"

She shook her head, vehemently. "I can't! The fire—I'm afraid it's going to get out of control soon."

A look of terror flashed on her face, yet she stayed rooted. Chase searched his memory. What had she said about her family losing a house to fire?

Grace gaped at Wren, then at the rising flames, and back to Chase. "I tried to lift her but she's dead weight."

He squatted next to Wren and checked her pulse, his expression grim. He called to Grace over his shoulder, "Before we lost power, I told your sisters to call the fire department. Any sign of them?"

"Oh, I was hoping they'd been called! Maybe I should look for them." Grace leaned over the railing, searching. The old wooden railing began to sway and Grace screamed. Chase leaped forward, wrapped an arm around her waist, and pulled her to safety.

Another rush of wind and heat caused the sweat on his face to drip off of his chin. The fire popped and a red-hot ember landed on the deck. Chase stomped it out with his heel and shouted, "Grace, go! Run to safety!"

Her body began to shake. "I'm not leaving you!"

He straightened and traced that beautiful, stubborn face of hers with his eyes. No woman had ever said anything so aggravating—and stunning—to him in his life. Ever.

He brushed his gaze across her lips, but tore his attention away, pulling his phone from his pocket. "Here, then. Help me see what I'm doing."

Grace grabbed his face with both hands and pressed her lips against his. They were soft ... forceful. Then she took his phone, switched on the flashlight, and raised it above him and Wren.

Chase had spent his life running as far from the flames as possible, but now, as the fire grew hotter, he found the strength to stay and fight back. Carefully, he lifted Wren into his arms and carried the ailing woman away from danger with Grace in the lead, lighting his path.

13

―――――

Darkness greeted the pair as they stepped inside the beach house. They'd been gone for hours and the electricity had yet to be restored.

The fire department had finally arrived and quickly extinguished the blaze beside Wren's home—but not before significant damage had been done to both the deck and the exterior wall from which it sprang.

"Poor Wren is going to have a mess to come home to," Grace said, wearily. She felt her way through the living room and into the kitchen. "I'm so thirsty. Can I get you some water?"

Chase followed her. "Yes, thanks." She handed him a bottle and he took a sip. "You were her savior tonight, you know."

"I wouldn't say that. You were the one who carried her down that dark staircase like a champ. I—I was so scared for her, Chase."

"Come here."

Instinctively, Grace reached for Chase. When she found him, she let her body sink into his embrace.

Though she had her suspicions, Grace didn't exactly know the cause of her sudden tears. The strain of the evening's events? Chase's sudden reappearance when she literally did not know what to do? Perhaps it was a little of both.

Whatever the cause, Grace's tears, uncharacteristic for her, flowed like a water spigot with its handle broken off.

Chase cupped the back of her head with his hands, his fingers lost in her mop of hair. She tried to pull back, to give him a way out of her emotions, but he held her tight, supporting her.

When her tears had stilled some, she tilted her head up. Her voice was thick. "What are we going to do, Chase?"

The question hung between them. He didn't bother to ask her what she meant—he knew. They had made a simple pact. He'd satisfy the requirements of his father's will and she would earn money for her wickedly high debts.

But the engagement turned into a hastily planned wedding.

An onboard reporter made their secret known.

They'd been lying to her family—and his—ever since.

Oh, and this one: They were not actually married.

Despite all the uncertainty, this she knew: his presence lit her senses, heating her through. Everything about his being here felt good, it felt right ... and she didn't want him to leave again. Ever.

But ...

Could she trust him with this intimate piece of her? Her heart? She swallowed back a harsh sigh. Why couldn't she just stop all the overthinking?

She sucked in a breath. "Chase—"

He found her mouth then, silencing her, his lips upon hers, as if answering her unspoken questions with one smoldering, bold, possessive ... kiss.

Her eyes had adjusted to the light enough to see the cloud of wanting in his eyes. A loop of warnings traveled through the synapses in her brain. He wanted her. She wanted him.

But where would that find them?

She cleared her throat and gently stepped back, shivering slightly.

His hands, thoroughly warm against her skin, rubbed the fleshy part of her upper arms. When she didn't make an effort to leave, he slid his hands down her body until they found the soft indent of her waist.

He tipped his head, pressing his forehead against hers, a slight sway to his hold on her. "Let's not tell anybody," he whispered.

"What? That you kissed me?"

"You kissed me first, you know."

She smiled in the darkness. "Are you saying we shouldn't tell anybody that we're not really married?"

He grinned. "I liked things the way they were before." He paused. "Didn't you?"

Grace closed her eyes, attempting to steady her breathing. It was as if she'd become locked into a tumbling position on a carnival cage ride.

When she didn't answer him, he said, "Is there something holding you back?"

She flashed a look at him, part of her wanting to wrap herself body and soul around him, and the other part ... petrified. Her parents had married for life and had committed themselves completely—body, mind, spirit. Was Chase ready to do that? Was she?

His hand at her waist loosened and he stepped back, creating a chasm between them. "Ah. I get it. You don't trust me."

A male voice coming from somewhere in the darkness sliced into their conversation. "Why should she trust you?"

Grace gasped.

Chase tensed and spun toward the voice, pulling Grace behind him in one powerful move.

But she broke free. "Jake?"

"You expecting somebody else?" her brother said.

"Well, I wasn't expecting you!"

"Clearly."

Chase cut in, "Were you ever going to let us know you were eavesdropping?"

"Was thinking about it." Jake got up from where he had likely been sprawled on the couch. Even in the dark, she could see the way he planted his feet solidly on the ground. He'd done that whenever he and their father went at it over his career choice.

Zeke let loose a scraggly bark, followed by a pitiful whine.

"You missing this?" Jake said and handed the dog to Grace, who tucked him quickly into the curl of her arm.

"Lotta help you are," she said to the animal. "Don't you know you're supposed to keep intruders out?"

"So about this predicament that you guys are in ..." Jake started.

Grace said, "How much did you hear?"

"Enough." Her brother threw a dagger-like look at

Chase. She'd seen that expression plenty of times too, enough to fill in the blanks created by the darkness.

"Jerk," she said under her breath.

Jake chuckled derisively. "It might help you to know that until a few minutes ago—around the time all that mauling and lip-smacking started—I had been asleep on Mom and Dad's lumpy old couch."

Chase put his arm around Grace's waist again, just as she readied herself to pounce on her brother, who had, obviously, not grown out of his teenage brain.

Chase said, "Listen, Jake. It's been a long night. We're both exhausted, but now that you're here," he paused, "I would like to clear up things for you about Grace and me. Right here. Right now."

Grace stuck a fist into her hip. "Wait a second, Chase." She hissed at her brother, "Spying on people is *illegal*, Jake!"

"So is your marriage. Apparently."

She refused to fall for his diversionary tactic. "You'd better tell me right now what you're doing here and why you hid from us."

Jake whistled, the sound of it not unlike their mother's when she whistled at something that most people just commented on. "In my defense, dear sister, I've been looking all over the place for you two. Neither of you answered your phones, by the way."

"In case you hadn't noticed, there's no power around here," Grace said, annoyingly mindful of the rising pitch of her voice. "We used up all the juice in our phones just to get Wren to safety, and neither of us thought about something as mundane as phone chargers when we were at the hospital waiting to hear if the poor woman would live or die!"

"Well, it's a good thing our good old neighbor had you to watch over her," he drawled.

"You're ridiculous. Why don't you like her?" Her brother's expression hardened whenever she mentioned Wren. And though she knew it would take some coaxing to find out why —if there even was a good reason—she couldn't help pushing him on the issue.

Jake scoffed, then glared at her.

Chase cut in, gently pulling Grace back from the edge. He put his arm around her, resting one hand lazily on her hip. "I'm calling a truce. Neutral corners for you both. I suggest we lock up this place—"

"So no more intruders get in?" Grace said, eyeing Jake in the shadows.

Chase turned her toward the hallway toward her bedroom. "So that we can all get some sleep tonight. We can talk about all this in the morning. Agreed?"

"Sure thing, pops," Jake said.

A shrill beep was followed by the return of electricity that lit the room. Unfortunately, someone had turned on every light in the place—likely Jake when he came home and found the place dark. The effect was stark, blinding.

They each stood in place, squinting slightly, and staring at each other. Zeke howled at some invisible moon.

Jake pursed his lips and glanced at his phone. He held it up for them all to see the screen. "More than a dozen texts from your sisters," he said. "They're asking if the power is back on."

"Why?"

"They want a do-over."

Grace scowled. "Now?"

"What do you mean, a do-over?" Chase asked.

Grace cast him a look. "They want to have another video call."

"Ah."

Jake stepped over to Grace's computer, which stood open from the earlier call. He slid a look at Grace. "Might want to brew a pot of coffee," he said. "My guess is this long night is about to get a lot longer."

HE'D NEVER LET the brother of any of his girlfriends get to him. Not that Chase had stuck around that long to meet many of them. But if he had, well, he'd have let their needling roll right down his back without even a glance.

But this was different. *She* was different.

And now he had four sets of eyeballs staring him down as if he was the big bad wolf and Grace was, well, Little Red Riding Hood.

He set his jaw, the nerves in his cheek sore.

"Grace should sue you for sexual harassment in the workplace!" Lacy said, smirking. Grace's ornery sister had been busy in the last few hours, it seemed. Her hair was piled up in some kind of beehive from the 50s. Her skin looked so slick with something shiny that he had to turn away. Whatever happened to splashing water on your face and hitting the sheets at the end of the day?

"I wasn't working for him when we entered into this agreement," Grace said, her teeth obviously clenched.

"Oh no?" Maggie said. "I talked to you when you were heading into work that morning, well, a morning before all this happened, I think. Were you not employed then? Or was that a lie too?"

Grace glanced at Chase, her eyes big and pleading. He resisted the urge to gather her up and charge out of there.

Chase expelled a breath. "Look. I was in a tough position. I told Grace that she no longer had a job with my firm—"

"You *fired* her?" Lacy scoffed. "Oh, that's rich. This is getting better and better ..."

He spoke through clenched teeth. "You should all be proud of your sister. She navigated my bad news with quick thinking and a savviness that impressed me. When I spilled my guts about my predicament, she offered her services."

Bella squealed and put her hand to her mouth, her eyes wide with shock.

Chase felt a smile try to surface. He looked at Bella. "Not *those* types of services."

Jake's scoff was harsh, audible. "From what I saw, that's not entirely true."

"You didn't see anything," Grace spat back.

"Pardon me. That's right. It was still dark in here. Let me rephrase that: from what I *heard* in here, that's not completely true."

Maggie frowned. "Ew."

"Yeah, get a room," Lacy said.

"Of all the stupid stunts, Grace. A fake marriage? Really?" Maggie was scowling, as usual, while simultaneously texting with who-knew-who.

Grace rubbed her hands vigorously on her lap. "You guys aren't listening! It was a simple business proposition. I suggested that I take on the role of his fiancée to get him out of a jam, and Chase paid me well to do so. It's no big deal to either of us and wasn't meant to hurt any of you—we've just been playing parts!"

Chase's gaze darted to Grace, whose face wore a mask of

incredulity. While she had been stirred to a frenzy by her siblings' obvious—and understandable—concern, she'd also managed to land a rocket punch to his gut.

Of course, he kept his expression stony. He'd been trained to keep his emotions in check for the courtroom, to not let the other guy see him sweat, so to speak.

Up until now, though, he hadn't actually been sweating.

His jaw did that clenching thing again.

Was she still play-acting? Even now?

Against his best judgment, Chase allowed his gaze to wander away from the screen with the bickering siblings and catch eyes with Grace. And when he did?

He knew.

GRACE AWOKE THE NEXT MORNING, her head throbbing like she'd tied one on the night before. She didn't wish a hangover on anyone, but frankly, that would have been preferable to last night's events.

She stared at the knotty pine ceiling, finding comfort in the familiar shapes from her past. She'd made her entire family angry last night—even Bella, it seemed—but she had also found home again. And her parents' love. And if she thought about it, even in their anger, she and her siblings had reconnected on some deeper level. That was a fine start.

And then there was Chase. He probably already left— he'd had that look on his face when they finally shut down the call and went into their respective corners, aka bedrooms. Thankfully, when it was over, her brother climbed the stairs and disappeared into their parents' room.

But she hadn't had a chance to tell Chase about her findings yet.

A screen door slammed.

A shout went out, followed by another—two different voices.

Grace sat up. She was too young to feel such achiness in her joints, so she pushed through it. Her feet hit the floor and she pulled on a robe while stifling a yawn. Then she padded over to the window that provided a slim view of the stairs that led to the sand and beyond.

She blinked and pressed her nose against the wavy glass.

Chase?

And Jake?

She pulled on a T-shirt and yoga pants. Then she coiled her hair up on her head, fastening it with a hair tie, and dashed a look in the mirror. That would have to do.

With a slight burst of energy, Grace hurried down the hall with Zeke yelping and drooling at her heels.

Outside, she leaned on the railing of the tiny back deck, marveling. Chase and her brother were spinning a disc at each other ... like children. Smiles big. Whoops going out. Hard landings in soft sand.

What in the world? What had transpired to suddenly make them ... allies?

"Duck!"

Grace lurched backward at the sight of a flying disc spinning straight toward her head. Unfortunately, Zeke was parked right behind her and she stepped on him, pulling back sharply so she wouldn't hurt him.

The dog yelped and Grace went flying—backward. She let out a scream and landed on her bum. Hard.

Before she could recapture her breath, Chase was on the floorboards of the deck, next to her.

He searched her face with earnest eyes. "Are you okay?"

That breath she'd lost? Yeah, she hadn't quite caught it yet.

She nodded.

"You always were a dork," her brother said.

Grace glared at Jake, though it was a rather fake glare. Would saying *I know you are but what am I?* be too cliché?

Jake threw his head back, laughing. Then he picked up the disc and whistled for Zeke. "C'mon, monster. You and I need to avert our eyes."

Zeke bounded down the steps, apparently able to switch loyalties in an instant.

Chase put his palm on the back of her head and gently released her hair from its scrunchie. He continued to watch her with serious eyes. "You sure you're okay?"

She managed a small smile. "Just embarrassed."

He helped her up. "Are you kidding? That disc could've done some damage. I'm glad you didn't take it in that beautiful face."

They were toe-to-toe now. While Grace was regretting her decision to practically roll out of bed and come outside, Chase leaned forward and kissed her.

"Good morning," he whispered, revealing the charm of crow's feet at the corners of his eyes. Then he kissed her again, taking his time with this one.

A satisfied little sigh rolled out of her of its own volition.

Chase stepped back, a smile still on his face. He reached a hand out to her. "Walk with me? We can stop at that bakery you like and get some coffee to revive you."

She pursed her lips, twisting a look his way. She glanced

at his hand. "I have to say something first. To, uh, come clean."

Chase frowned. "Go on."

She blew out a breath, calmed herself, then looked him in the eye. "When I accepted the position with the firm, I didn't mention that I needed a month off right away."

"I see."

"I desperately needed the job and hoped something could be worked out. Only I hadn't had the chance to figure out what that would be exactly. I'm sorry for not owning up to the truth when you asked me about it." She watched his lawyer face, the one that masked his emotions, take over. "Say something, Chase. What are you thinking?"

He stared for a long beat, his eyes laser-focused on her, and she held her breath as the seconds of quiet dragged on. Finally, he said. "I'm thinking ... well, right now I'm wondering if that bakery has any muffin tops left today. Sure could use a couple."

She released a breath and quirked a smile at him. "So ... I'm forgiven?"

He grinned and reached out his hand again, which she took this time without further comment. As they began down the beach together, Chase shook his head, muttering, "A month-long vacation before your probationary period even ended—"

"Chase!"

He chuckled as they walked along, hand in hand.

The tide was out, providing them with level, wet sand to feel beneath their feet. For the first time in a long while, Grace leaned into the moment, not wishing it to end. Her mind wandered back to when she had awakened to find

Chase and her brother running around outside like teenagers in the morning light.

"So ... what broke the ice between you and Jake?"

Chase shrugged and looked out to sea. "Oh, I don't know. I think he just realized that I'm not the man he'd conjured up in his head."

"Oh, yeah? And who was that?"

He swung a look at her. "A cad. A playboy. Some guy who didn't have his sister's best interest in mind."

She stopped. "And you do?"

He took both of her hands and pulled her around until they faced each other. "Yes, ma'am."

"I see."

He grinned, then his expression turned sober. He dropped his gaze and then looked up. "I'm not going to fight Kate for the clients."

Grace halted. "Excuse me?"

"She can have them."

She searched his face. "But why?"

"Doesn't matter."

"Wait. What is it?"

He gave his head a slight shake, his smile sad. "I didn't tell you this, but it was Kate who discovered that we weren't legally married. I confirmed it with Judge Cape."

"So ... ?"

"So she's threatening to go to Peter with a sordid spin on our union. I can't let her do that to you, Grace." His jaw visibly tightened. "I won't."

"You can't let Peter go! He's been your father's client for— what?—thirty years?"

"Sshh." He cupped her shoulders, cinching her closer.

"Maybe I'd like to start something new," he said, leaning his forehead against hers, "with you."

She steadied her breath. "I'd like that."

"Then it's all settled."

She closed her eyes and breathed him in, trying to focus on the levity of his decision while not succumbing completely, body and soul, to his embrace.

"Chase," she whispered, "no way. You have to fight. I'm in this with you."

"That's great to know, Grace. It is. But I already called her this morning." He inhaled, pulling her closer still. "I'll be meeting her this week to hand over the files."

Without pulling away, Grace snapped a look up at him. "Well, then, maybe you'll just have to hand her something else entirely."

Chase frowned. "I don't understand."

Grace wrapped her arms around him, raised on her tiptoes, and kissed his neck, lingering in the warmth. "Chase, I have a surprise for you. But you'll have to get me coffee and a muffin top first."

CHASE HAD KNOWN that Grace was smart. But devious? That had surprised him.

After they'd stopped for coffee and breakfast at the bakery, after they'd passed by the little church that she had waxed poetic about, he left her at the beach house to think about what she'd done.

A grin that he was unable to contain spread across his face. When he told Grace he was giving everything up for her, she'd balked. She'd urged him not to do so. And then she showed him something she'd been working on —for him.

What a fighter.

He drove his SUV down the tree-lined road that ended at a condominium complex on the west side of LA. Parking wasn't going to be easy—never was around here. He pulled a U-turn mid-block, just as a spot opened up.

He didn't want to be here, but then again, Grace's little secret had made the whole experience more ... palatable.

Chase knocked on the door, and characteristically, Kate made him wait a full minute before answering. She stared at him like he was prey. "Come in."

"Hello to you, too," he said.

Kate clucked her tongue. "There's coffee if you want it." She turned. "Is that hospitable enough for you?"

"I take mine with cream, not sugar. Of course, you already know that."

"If you want anything else you're going to have to have it delivered." Then she poured him a cup and slid it across the counter toward him. It tasted bitter.

"So," she said, eyeing the slim folder in his arms, "you're not going to try to tell me that file contains all of Mayer's documents."

"No, I'm not."

"I figured as much. There must be a horde of boxes in the storeroom, though why you never had them scanned and put on a flash drive years ago is beyond irresponsible."

"Worked for my father all those years."

"Hmm."

"By the way, Judith hired an outside firm to do a detailed analysis of our billing invoices. No one was overcharged." He paused. "But you knew that."

She shrugged. "What's done is done."

"As in, the damage you've done."

"Whatever."

He looked at her, more thoughtfully now. Kate had always been a beauty to him, but today he noted the deep crevice between her eyes, the tautness of her lips as they stretched into a thin, hard line ... the way she drummed her fingers impatiently on her kitchen counter.

She flashed a look at the file folder he carried. "So what is that? Your audit?" She laughed as she said it.

He shook his head grimly. Then slid the file toward her.

She snatched it up, pursed her lips, and flipped it open, her expression moving from studious to severe. Her eyes flashed at him. "What is this?"

His flashed back. "It's self-explanatory."

She smacked the file back onto the counter. "It's blackmail."

"It's the truth."

"It was a joke!"

"I don't think Peter Mayer would find seeing you in a devil's getup very funny. Lotta red in that. Oh, and that pitchfork!"

"You know very well that this was one of my dance routines!"

He chuckled. "Oh, so that's what we're calling it now."

"It was all in fun, Chase. The other dance students will testify to that."

"Somehow I don't think Mayer will care. He's a devout Christian and even the perception that his attorney is associated with the dark side will dissuade him, I'm sure."

"It was pretend, like your marriage."

"I somehow doubt Mayer would consider dancing with Satan as something to joke about."

Kate set her jaw, her eyes ablaze. "What do you want?"

"I want you to keep your findings about my marriage to Grace to yourself." He didn't have to add that, otherwise, he stood to lose everything ... even though he knew he was about to gain so much.

"And if I do?"

"I won't share my findings with my billionaire client."

"You mean, *my* billionaire client."

"If Peter decides to go with your firm, I won't try to stop him."

The tension in her expression softened some, though the finger tapping continued. "I can make that work."

He could tell that the fight had left her. Compromise was not her strength, but she knew that without it, she'd not get her way.

And she hated that.

GRACE HAD PACKED up most of her things the night before. She glanced out the picture window, taking in the gleam of satiny waves. The sun would be setting soon, and so the nightly appearance of locals had begun.

Chase had been gone all week, but he'd promised to return for one last call with her siblings. Considering how poorly the last one had ended, she wasn't looking forward to it.

Then again, Chase and Jake had forged some kind of weird guy bond. She shook her head, unable to stop smiling at the thought of them tossing a Frisbee on the beach like, well, like brothers.

The phone rang and she dove for it, nearly tripping over Zeke again. *Hopefully, nobody saw that ...* "Hello?"

"Yes, hello. This is Lillian Madsen calling from Madsen Realty and Investments. May I speak with Ms. Holloway?"

Grace shut her eyes. A Realtor. She remembered the woman the moment she'd said her full name. Grace had been so wound up about seeing Chase, that she had not checked Caller I.D. "This is she."

"Wonderful! I remember when your family would summer here in Colibri Beach. Delightful couple. Please accept my condolences."

"Yes. Of course. Thank you."

"Now, I would like to visit with you soon to talk about your plans for the beach house. Would tomorrow at one o'clock in the afternoon fit your schedule?"

The front door opened and she spun around.

"I'm here," Chase said.

"You're here!"

Lillian interrupted her. "Excuse me? I'm not there, but I could be—"

Grace turned back to the phone, shaking her head. "No. I'm sorry, Lillian, but you'll have to excuse me."

"But it is imperative—"

"Goodbye now." Grace hung up and turned her attention to Chase, who stepped across the room, eyes on her, and kissed her swiftly.

She inhaled him. "You smell good."

"I'll have to remember to shower every day then." He held a tease in his voice. Zeke yapped and danced at his feet until the poor man bent down and gave the pup a proper rubdown.

Chase stood up again and Grace gave him a tentative smile. "So."

"So?"

"You said you had some news?"

"The news is I'm inundated with business and I don't see an end in sight."

"Really? Oh, I'm so happy for you!" She hugged him quickly. "So I guess this means that the loss of those big clients to Kate hasn't hurt you."

He grinned. "I haven't lost any clients to Kate."

"Wait. What?"

"Peter decided to keep his corporation with me."

She squealed, then threw her arms around his neck and hugged him, tighter this time.

He laughed. "Guess I forgot to mention that."

She rolled her eyes. "You think?"

Chase looped an arm around her waist. "It's been an amazing week, Grace. First, Mayer stays, and once that news spread, it created a domino effect. Former clients have been calling all week, wanting to reinstate me as their attorney. Several mentioned that they took a close look at their invoices and realized that Kate had been blowing smoke." He chuckled. "And one said, 'If that goody-two-shoes Mayer trusts you, then so do I!'"

"Wow, this is all so amazing, Chase. Congratulations!"

"Couldn't have done it without you," he said, his voice husky.

She smiled up at him. "Yeah?"

"She backed down—way down—after seeing the photo you'd found." He chuckled when he said it.

A text dinged her phone. Reluctantly, she pulled her gaze from Chase and checked the screen. "Oh! It's Maggie." She broke away from him and jogged over to her computer, which was set up on the kitchen table next to her computer bag. She threw a glance over her shoulder. "You had me so distracted that I'm late for our call."

Chase shrank back. "Me?"

She laughed and swatted the air between them. "Get over here."

Maggie was the first to show, then Lacy, followed by Bella, and then Jake.

"I think we should set some ground rules for these calls," Maggie said.

"Oh, pshaw," Lacy said, a mimosa in her hand. "Last week's was the most fun I've had with my family in years."

Bella cracked up at this.

Grace cut in. "I don't think we need any ground rules. Last week's call was weird, I'll grant you that. We were exhausted from dealing with Wren and the fire and, you know, all the stuff."

Jake chortled. "Yeah, I know about the 'stuff.'" He air-quoted the word.

Grace glared at him, but it was playful this time.

Maggie interrupted. "How is Wren, by the way?"

"She's been moved to a rehab facility, but from what I understand, she should be fine. Can't get back into the house for a long while, though. Not until repairs are made."

Bella frowned. "Poor Wren. Is there anyone who can help her?"

Lacy gaped at Jake, but he looked away.

Grace continued, "I talked to Wren. She says her daughter, who's a world traveler, is coming to see her, so my guess is that she'll take over."

Jake frowned. "Isn't her daughter a little kid?"

"Yeah, like a million years ago," Lacy said. "Sheesh, Jake."

"I remember her," Bella said.

"Glad to hear it," Maggie said. "Good to know Wren won't be alone to navigate the permitting process at the city. Dad always complained about how ignorant those people were."

"Ha. Dad was right," Lacy said.

Jake, who'd had his share of dealing with planning issues, managed to keep quiet through the back-and-forth. Grace's mind wandered to when they were teens and she'd watched her father and Jake argue.

"Surprised to see you on this call, Chase," Lacy said, "especially since you're not exactly a member of this family anymore."

"I'd like to be."

All eyes turned to him.

Grace tilted her head, her mind muddled with the chaos of her musings mixed with her siblings' constant questions. "Would like to be what?"

He grinned. Her siblings fell silent, all except for Bella who elicited a slight, high-pitched gasp.

Grace gave everyone a half-frown. "Did I miss something?"

Chase took her hand, his grin growing wider still, and he kissed her fingers. His Adam's apple bobbed and his gaze sobered. He dropped to one knee.

Bella squealed again and Lacy uttered, "What in the world?" Maggie shushed them both.

Emotion filled Chase's eyes in a way Grace had never

seen before. "You've surprised me, challenged me, and from what I've been told—undone me," he said. "Marry me. For real this time. In that little church, with all the trimmings."

"It needs paint ..."

"We'll paint it."

She laughed, not sure if she truly understood what was happening. A sudden shadow crossed her mind. "Your father ..."

But Chase continued to grin. "Will be in attendance, full of health, it seems."

Grace reached down and stroked his cheek. "That would be so wonderful, but ..."

"My father's memory problems were determined to have been brought on by too much medication, Grace."

She gasped.

"I've been wanting to tell you," he said. "Dad's doing far better now, and his prognosis is good."

Tears dripped down Grace's cheeks. "Honey, that's the best news I've heard all day."

"Reason one-hundred-and-one why I love you so much." Chase reached into his pocket and lifted a white box, flipping it open to display a gorgeous diamond winking up at her. He looked into her eyes. "I adore you, Grace. This one's for keeps."

She gawked at him and the ring in his hands, the very breath in her chest stilled. Her mind spun through her thoughts like a computer searching for a file. She'd been planning to end this call quickly, to throw her bags into Chase's SUV, and to head home to the quiet walls of her small apartment with Zeke in tow.

She had not thought much about what would happen after that.

"Oh, for heaven's sake, Grace," Lacy said. "You're killing us here."

Both Maggie and Bella shushed her. To his credit, Jake kept his thoughts to himself.

Grace's mouth broke into a smile. She laughed. "Yes, of course, I'll marry you!"

Then Chase pulled her down to him, far out of view of the webcam, and kissed her like a starving man who had just been served a three-course meal. They tumbled to the floor in an embrace, Zeke's hot breath on their cheeks, their laughter intertwined.

Jake's voice broke in, his drawl lazy. "Sounds like it did the other night."

"Jake!" Bella scolded.

"Get a room—stat!" Lacy said, her laughter light.

"Um, excuse me ... Chase? Grace?" Maggie, as usual, tried to restore order.

Chase stood and pulled Grace up, keeping his hand linked with hers. He looked into the webcam, smiling. "She said yes, guys." He lifted her hand to his mouth and kissed it again.

"We gathered that," Maggie said. "Congratulations, you two, though it feels like we were just saying that not too long ago."

Grace's smile was sheepish. "Again, sorry about that."

"Oh, I'm so excited for you guys," Bella said, her voice wistful. "Will you be going on a real honeymoon? Now that you're, you know, really getting married?"

Chase glanced at his fiancée, a mischievous gleam in his eyes. "Absolutely. Anywhere ... but on a boat."

Laughter flowed through the room, bouncing, joyful laughter, just like it often had when they were kids, far before they had their own worries to obsess about. It occurred to her that they had, somehow, found a bit of that again.

When her parents had left the Holloway kids the beach house, they'd all been confounded by the rule that each one had to stay a month before they all decide what to do with the place.

As Grace took in the faces of her siblings, their expressions filled with wonder and laughter and curiosity, she began to understand.

"Jake," Grace said, "I'm passing the baton to you. It's your turn to start your month of memories at the beach house." She paused. "So get your booty down here already!"

Another whoop of laughter went up inside the family's old beach house. Then Chase pulled Grace even farther from view, away from gaping eyes, and kissed her in a way that was anything but ... fake.

ALSO BY JULIE CAROBINI

Julie's books are available wherever books are sold, including her online shop: JulieCarobini.com

<u>Beach House Romances</u>

Beach Sunrise (book 1)

Beach Memories (book 2)

Beach Secrets (book 3)

Beach Sunset (book 4)

Beach Music (book 5)

<u>Standalone</u>

Reunion in Saltwater Beach

<u>Hollywood by the Sea Novels</u>

Chasing Valentino (book 1)

Finding Stardust (book 2)

<u>Sea Glass Inn Novels</u>

Walking on Sea Glass (book 1)

Runaway Tide (book 2)

Windswept (book 3)

Beneath a Billion Stars (book 4)

A Sea Glass Christmas (book 5)

<u>**Otter Bay Novels**</u>

Sweet Waters (book 1)

A Shore Thing (book 2)

Fade to Blue (book 3)

The Otter Bay Novel Collection (books 1-3)

<u>**The Chocolate Series**</u>

Chocolate Beach (book 1)

Truffles by the Sea (book 2)

Mocha Sunrise (book 3)

<u>**Cottage Grove Cozy Mysteries**</u>

The Christmas Thief (book 1)

The Christmas Killer (book 2)

The Christmas Heist (book 3)

Cottage Grove Mysteries (books 1-3)

ABOUT THE AUTHOR

JULIE CAROBINI is the author of 22+ inspirational beach romances. Her books feature captivating heroines, endearing heroes, and a cast of quirky friends, all bound together by the secrets they hold. Her bestselling titles include *Walking on Sea Glass, Runaway Tide,* and *Reunion in Saltwater Beach.* Julie has received awards for writing and editing from The National League of American Pen Women and ACFW, and she is a double finalist for the ACFW Carol Award. She is the mother of three grown kids and lives on the California coast with her husband, Dan, and their rescue pup, Dancer.

Please visit her at
www.juliecarobini.com